Binding of the Almatraek

Book Three:

Enchanted Page

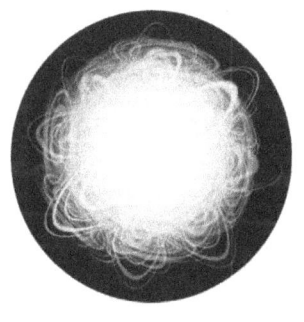

Heather Reilly

Published by Reilly Books
at Createspace
www.reillybooks.com

ISBN: 978-0-9939758-2-0

Other Novels by the author:
Binding of the Almatraek
Book I: Knight's Surrender

Binding of the Almatraek
Book II: Noble Pursuit

Children's Storybooks:
The Tree and the Sun

Tock Tick Tock,
The Mouse and the Clock

The Poetical Alphabetical Book

Santa Almost Missed Our Town (illustrations)

Games:
Cauldron Cards

Upcoming books:
The Rat of Red Vine

The Words We See:
Kindergarten Sight Words on the Rock

To learn more about the author or her books, visit

www.reillybooks.com
www.amazon.com
ebooks: www.smashwords.com

Dedication

This book is dedicated to all of you adventurers who have joined me in every step of this tale. Thank you for your ongoing support.

And the puns...they were for you, Dave.

Acknowledgments

I would like to thank, Ian, from a living history group called La Belle Compagnie, who helped me greatly with respect to understanding armour from the era this book takes place in. Please take the time to visit their website at:

http://www.peelaffinity.net/?page_id=79

to learn more about what they do, and the presentations they make to educate those of all ages about life, combat, and armour in the thirteen and fourteen hundreds.

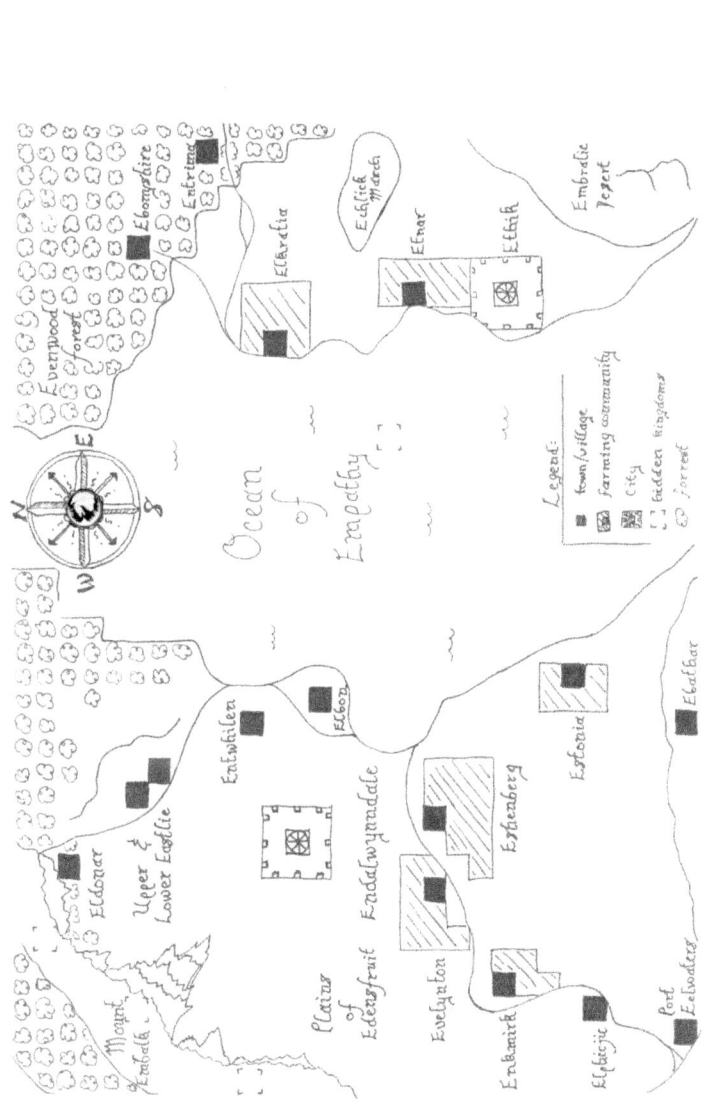

Chapter 1
☼ A Dream ☼

Cast yourself back to a time when Endalwynndale was still in turmoil. Aurastia and Zaltreous threaten our subjects with the dark magic held within the *Almatraek Dim*. The new king is about to leave the throne to partake in a quest to capture a rare magic item to help him conquer those foes. But will it be enough? There is a book of antidotes and counter spells they desperately need, and one brave mage has volunteered to help them find it.

*　　　*　　　*

Lazelan awoke to the warm bright sunlight streaming in through the windows of the little cottage he owned with his new wife, Magdolyn. He felt awful. He had overslept, but the panic of being late was dulled by the grogginess he felt. It was no real wonder. He had been up late, planning his trip right into the wee hours of the morning while he went over a list of all of the provisions he thought he might need.

He had been scried by Aylan and Oslan, his old friends and new rulers across the Ocean of Empathy. They had told him of their plight, and he had agreed to leave on the morrow for his quest to find the *Almatraek Bright*. That would be today, and it seemed that he would begin his quest under a heavy shroud of exhaustion.

He could hear Maggie's sweet song, and the sound of a wooden spoon dully thudding against a bowl in the other room as she served their morning meal of porridge.

He sighed and resisted getting out of bed.

He thought back to when he and Magdolyn had met at a tavern while attending the university in Ethik many years ago. She had patiently waited for him to complete his years of studies and work for the old king until he could return to her from Endalwynndale. He had not had many opportunities over those long years to visit, but they had written to each other daily. Every time the castle messenger would come to him with a letter, his heart would race with excitement to see the graceful loop of her hand. He knew that while he was away, many had pestered her about why she waited for him, but he also knew that time apart made the heart grow fonder. They were more in love now than they had ever been. When he had returned, he had gladly taken her as his wife, and for a short time, they had been truly happy.

Now though, he knew she was furious with him. She *had* been patient to wait for him all those years, and now that he had returned home, she wanted him to stay put. She had objected hotly about the new trip he was about to undertake.

What made it worse was that he could not tell her when he would return. He had no idea where his journey would take him as he sought the *Almatraek Bright*, one of two great leather-bound tomes of magic. It was the only thing that contained counter spells and antidotes for the evil magic of the *Almatraek Dim* that was currently a threat to those he held dear.

The royal family he had served in Endalwynndale was in danger, and he could not turn his back on the kingdom that had been so kind to him. Years ago, he had been on a journey for the university in Ethik when his boat had succumbed to a violent storm. Clutching a broken piece of the ship, he had survived the rest of the storm, and then had begun to swim. After exhausting himself, he simply floated on his back, looking up at the clouds that seemed to drift as peacefully as he. At length, he was spotted by some fishermen who pulled him aboard as he finally lost consciousness. They brought him to their shores and the former king, Eurilas, who had taken Lazelan in, given him clothes, shelter, and a job as the kingdom's mage.

Lazelan felt it was his duty to go, and since he was the head of the household, Maggie simply had no say in the matter. Unfortunately, it *was* within her power to give him the silent treatment. He had not heard the voice he had ached for years to hear for two days now, and if he wanted to be honest with himself, he was still in bed so he could avoid the glare of her angry eyes. He listened to the notes she sang as she worked, the cadence of her song rising and falling as if on the waves of a lulling sea.

After a few minutes at peace, the nagging feeling that his tardiness evoked forced him out of bed. He resigned himself to get ready, and threw back the covers that had been creating his warm and cozy nightly cocoon. The cool air woke him fully as it stole the warmth from his skin. He quickly slipped out of his bed and into the light flowing clothes he had set out for the hot day ahead. At the sound of his stirring, her singing sharply cut off. *Stubborn woman!* He thought to himself as he tried to tame his curly red hair by combing his fingers through it. He packed two more outfits into his satchel, and left their bedroom.

She crossed the tiny kitchen before him, eyes plastered to the bowls she carried. He knew she was making a point of not looking at him. If she did, she might see the hurt in his eyes, and fold. He approached her, and her body stiffened. He wrapped his long arms around her and tenderly kissed her cheek.

"I love you with all my heart," he told her, "Thank you for breakfast."

She endured the embrace until he released her, then went about her business without showing a sign that he was in the same room.

He sighed and sat down to his meal. It cut him to the bone and made his heart ache that she could be so cold, but he couldn't blame her. He was relieved when he heard a knock at the door, and a breathless Rebekkah entered.

"Is he gone yet?" she asked in a rush, then spotting him, finished with: "Oh."

Lazelan bent his head low over his meal and ate more quickly, feeling like a scolded dog with its tail between its legs.

Rebekkah was Magdolyn's best friend, and he was glad that she had agreed to stay with his wife for the duration of his trip. He knew she was on Maggie's side in this whole business, and that it would be best for him to leave before he had to feel the sharp side of her tongue.

He finished his porridge, rose from the table, and ducked into the strap of his satchel. Along with his clothes, it held some more food, notes he had taken when researching the two giant books, some potions, pastes and pills that Aylan, his former pupil, had gifted him upon his leaving Endalwynndale, a bowl and cutlery, and tools for writing Maggie as he travelled. Being as proficient as he was with wielding magic energy, he needed very little else.

He returned to the bedroom and found a reprieve from Rebekkah's judging stare, *at least she'll look at me,* he thought sardonically, and folded his magical travelling cloak. It was a curious thing, but a powerful tool. It looked like a normal cloak, billowing down to his ankles, with a deep hood that would conceal most of his face if needed. Its colour was a deep velvety burgundy, with embroidered golden suns that stood out as a trim along the edge of the hood and the front where the cloak closed. In case of an attack, magical or otherwise, this simple fabric would act as a shield that even an arrow could not penetrate. It went into his pack. He attached a bedroll to the outer straps of his bag, and added a coil of rope. He was ready.

He rejoined the two women and gave Rebekkah a nod, "Rebekkah, thank you for coming." To which she crossed her arms in front of her chest and nodded back grudgingly. He walked to the door near where Magdolyn stood. He didn't waste time with pleading with her or apologizing. The time for that had long past and had yielded no fruit anyway.

Instead, he embraced her in a flash, pulling her off balance to force her to hold onto him in order to save herself from going down. He would never have let her fall; he dipped her low to the ground and planted a kiss firmly and deeply onto her startled parted lips. A traitorous giggle escaped from her as in surprise, she started kissing him back. Then she realized that she had been bamboozled and ended it. The stern look she gave him cracked though, when he told her again that he loved her.

"I love you too," she replied, "of course, you know that. Be careful, and come back to me with all of your limbs still in-tact."

"I will." He promised simply. He righted her and placed another tender kiss on her forehead before releasing her and setting out. *And I seriously hope that that is a promise I can keep,* he inwardly prayed, but his tummy felt like the contents of a butter churn.

Chapter 2
✪ Great Balls of Fire ✪

Lazelan felt melancholy as he walked down the road that meandered through town. He passed the friendly faces of those working in their gardens or hanging washing on their lines. Many of them stopped their chores to wave a greeting and enquire about his day. As he drew near the edge of town, he realized how fond of Ethik he was. A brief wave of homesickness turned his stomach, and he had to squash the urge to run home to Maggie that instant.

I'll be fine, he tried to convince himself. *I'll get back home just as soon as I can.* He hoped he was successful for his friends' sake, but he also knew that if he was, it would mean that a longer trip would be needed to return the book to Endalwynndale. Although, perhaps he could persuade Maggie to go with him then, to his knowledge, she had never been outside the borders of Ethik. They had never travelled together, and he was growing fonder of the idea by the minute. He was daydreaming about this happy idea when he came to the edge of town, and crossed out into the world.

He continued to follow the road north past the fields and farms of their neighboring town of Etnar. He really had no leads to go on as to where to even begin looking for the *Almatraek Bright*, so Lazelan decided that the best person to ask was one of his professors from the university that knew much about the history and origins of magic. He was a monk, but not in the traditional sense.

Harmonium Magster had studied magic for so long that folks had lost count of his years and no longer knew how old he really was. What made it harder to figure out was the fact that he appeared to be a man in his forties; old enough for these times, however, he had looked this age for the last sixty years.

Beyond that, there were only tales of his exploits as a younger mage, and fantastic they were. Harmonium was a mystery, but had become a good friend that Lazelan believed he could trust.

He rounded the last bend of the uneven wheel-ruts that served as the farmers' dirt road between the towns, and saw the smoke that would undoubtedly be rising from the chimney of Harmonium's home. On this side of the Ocean of Empathy, the kingdom was always hot to the point that even the afternoon breezes did little to cool the sweat from your brow. Even so, Harmonium always had his hearth fire blazing, for the man insisted on always having hot tea at hand. Lazelan shook his head and chuckled to himself at the quirk. It was hard to fault a man for his habits when he had managed to stay alive so long in doing them.

Lazelan saw the red roof first. Curved crescent shaped shingles laid in layer upon layer climbed to the house's tall peak, only to be broken by the chimney that rose on one side. Sure enough, Lazelan noted the grey-white smoke that billowed lazily out the chimney top. He approached the large stone house, bleached white by either time or magic, and called out for Harmonium instead of knocking. He knew the monk often spent a good deal of his time outside in back of the house training his body and magic. As he suspected he would, Lazelan heard a reply come from around the structure.

"Lazelan, my boy, come around to the back!" the fatherly voice called. Lazelan followed the sound until he came to the tall peonies that grew as a wall around his backyard. Again Lazelan smiled at the oddities of the older man. Harmonium had come across the peonies when travelling to the cooler side of the kingdom, and had fallen in love with the pink and white blooms. He had brought them with him when he had returned home, despite warnings that it was too hot for them to grow on this side of the ocean. Oh, but they had thrived. Especially since Harmonium had created a magic atmosphere over his garden that they would love.

There was no discernible way into the back yard. Harmonium had once told Lazelan that if a mage couldn't even think their way into a yard with no door, they would be simply wasting his time in being there. He required that any students needing to visit his home have both brains and magical ability. This one had been easy for Lazelan the first time he had arrived here. He drew energy from his core just like he had done on that first visit, and simply said "Fli." *Levitate.* The spell fed off of his energy and he rose into the air, up and over the flowers.

Landing deftly on the other side, Lazelan immediately dropped his things, and threw up a shield of magic. A large ball of fire two feet across slammed into him, throwing him backward. As the dynamism of the fireball forced him across the backyard, he felt the tremendous heat lick up his arms, and cause sweat to burst out in droplets along his brow. He thudded to the ground, sliding another three feet, and feeling like he had been kicked by a horse. The fireball dissipated as quickly as it had been formed, and Lazelan felt goose-bumps rise on his skin from the sudden lack of intense heat. Thanks to the shield, he had been left unsigned, but he was still forced to pick himself up and dust off his clothes.

"May brightness guide you," he groaned in a

pained voice as his usual greeting to Harmonium, who stood thirty feet away and approached quickly. The sun gleamed off his bald head, and Lazelan had to squint slightly as he drew near. It wouldn't have been so bad, but the monk was short and built like a wall, and as he stooped to gather Lazelan's things the glare was pronounced.

"And you." Harmonium jovially responded back. He handed Lazelan his things and stood, bare chested, fists on hips, sweating despite the coolness of the garden's atmosphere. *Figures,* Lazelan thought, *that I would catch him in the middle of a training session. Then again, when does the man ever stop?*

"Must we do this every time?" Lazelan questioned wearily.

"I thought you might have grown soft in that cushy job of yours at the palace. I just wanted to keep you on your toes." Harmonium answered a little too innocently.

"But instead," Lazelan insisted, "you knocked me *off* my toes."

"Indeed. I'm glad I can still sweep you off your feet, although, I would prefer if you were a dark haired beauty of the female persuasion." The older man said with a wink. "Your training will never be complete if a measly fireball will put you down, Lazelan," Harmonium pointed out. He surveyed the other mage's things, and asked "Are you going on a trip?"

"I am, and I have come to you for guidance" Lazelan informed him.

"Don't go, that's my advice. Home is where the heart is." Harmonium said, gesturing with his thickly corded arm to his vast training ground of a back yard. The walls were made of peonies down both sides of the long expanse, and a wooden trellis covered in some sort of vine created shade over part of the yard. Near the house there was a wooden table and small pond full of fish of different colours. Straw mats made up an even floor, and at the far end of the yard there stood a stone wall covered in scorch marks. This is where Harmonium meditated and practiced his personal brand of offensive magic.

"I go in search of the *Almatraek Bright*, have you heard of it?" Lazelan asked.

"Do mongrels have fleas?" he retorted, with a look that said the younger mage should know better. "Have a seat, Lazelan, I have just the tea for this."

With that, Harmonium disappeared into his house and emerged moments later with two piping hot cups of tea. Their discussion lasted until the shadow of the peonies had shifted and shrank, and had begun to elongate once again. It was past the hour for diner by the time they had finished deciding where the best place would be to start. Lazelan had decided it was best to go to the last place that Harmonium knew the book had travelled. It had likely moved on from there, but the people there would have the best recollection of it, and may be able to give him the best lead. He just hoped that they would prove to be helpful, and not try to hinder him in order to protect the book.

Chapter 3
☼ Horsing Around ☼

Harmonium once again emerged from the house, this time balancing a platter of bread, cheese, fish, and even some fruit. After their long morning discussion, it was a welcomed sight. Lazelan's tummy rumbled.

"I'm sorry for keeping you so long, my friend," Harmonium apologized, "but this really will work out for the better. You don't want to head into the desert when the sun is still high just after noon. Eat first and then start on your journey." Within the cooler expanse of garden, Lazelan had almost forgotten that the outside world would be uncomfortably hot. The thought of entering the desert when the sun was sweltering made him second guess his plan. *I've got to start thinking farther ahead.* He realized. Though without knowing where he would end up, it was hard to do so.

"It might be wise," Harmonium suggested, "for us to create some packets that will flare in the dark. That at least you can be ready for, as the night time is inevitable."

Lazelan agreed. Harmonium moved their empty dish to the other side of the table and pointed him toward a long box with a lid that swung upward. Inside, Lazelan found vials, pouches, bottles, and jars of ingredients used to create magic packets. Harmonium lifted a small satchel of something out of the box and handed it up for Lazelan to see. The young mage gently squeezed and smelled the packet to see what it might contain. He couldn't tell. He decided to open it and take a look inside. Within the pouch was a fine dust that sparkled under the light.

"Diamond dust, I'd bet my life on it." Lazelan concluded. Harmonium smiled and continued taking other herbs out of the box to set before the younger mage. Lazelan opened a few smaller satchels that would become his flare packets. He began adding ingredients, and Harmonium returned them to their places in the box.

Above them, an unnoticed shiny black spider dangled from a web. Lengthening its thread of silk, the spider silently dropped into one of Lazelan's tiny satchels. Looking at the spider wriggling through the dust, he wondered *Will this even still work? We have no idea what effect this will have. It would be better to start over and get rid of this one.* He sighed and showed the pouch to Harmonium, who gently took the spider out and placed it on a nearby bloom.

"This mixture will be too dangerous to use," the monk advised, thinking about the particles that might have fallen off of the spider into the satchel, "but the rest should serve you well."

As they worked, Harmonium had explained that nestled amongst the dry and barren sand dunes of the Embralic Desert, was a pyramid that served as a fortress for the princess of the desert people. It was completely enclosed and not one window allowed for weakness to a foe. Harmonium's grey eyes sobered when he warned Lazelan about the pyramid being booby-trapped. "If you should get within the walls, you will be faced with very real danger, my friend."

Lazelan looked off into space. He began to realize what an undertaking this quest would be. Harmonium brought his attention back to the present.

"But that is enough talk for one day, for I know that you wish to embark." With that, Harmonium cleared the remnants of their meal and retreated into the house.

Harmonium was gone for a while, and Lazelan began to think that he had been dismissed, though it was strange that his friend had forgotten to wish him well on his journey. Although Lazelan was not a superstitious man, it still felt odd to be leaving without his friend's blessing. He began to gather his things when Harmonium returned with some wrapped packages of food that he handed to Lazelan.

"Thank you my friend," Lazelan said in relief as he accepted the bundles and added them and the flare satchels to his pack. Harmonium waved off his gratitude and walked to the middle of the training ground.

"Step back, would you Lazelan? Harmonium requested. "This is the quickest way of watering my garden." The bald man walked to the center of his training space, and took up a battle stance. With legs apart and knees bent, bringing his center of gravity closer to the ground, he brought his wrists together, spread his palms apart, and began to produce a ball of magic. It was blue crackling energy, and as it got bigger, he moved his stance, wrists still together, so that his open palms pointed upward toward the sky above his head. With one thundering word: "Oatasa!" *Rain!* he launched the ball upwards into the clear blue sky above. The air began to swirl and clouds began to form as water vapour from the air gathered around the force of magic. The particles grew heavier until they started to drop from the heavens.

Harmonium spread his hands and called out another spell: "Falfakti", *Shield*. A clear bubble erupted from his palms and spread out over the interior of the back yard. It stopped at the peonies and house, which were left uncovered. The fabricated rain fell from the sky, landing all over the garden. As more water gathered and fell, the electric ball in the sky grew smaller and smaller, as its energy was expended. Eventually, the water stopped, and Harmonium dropped his shield spell, allowing it to dissipate. Water gleamed on the leaves of the peonies. The flowers, now heavy with rain, bent toward the ground.

Lazelan just gaped in astonishment under the lip of roof that jutted out from the back of Harmonium's house.

"There. Now let's go to the stable, for such a journey requires a horse. I have just the one for you." Harmonium told him, chuckling.

They both used levitation spells to leap out over the opposite side of the garden. A worn dirt path led to another white stone building with a red roof. This is where Harmonium kept his stables, which housed several fine horses. To his surprise, two beasts were saddled and one was laden with supplies the average person would need for a long trip.

"Oh, no," Lazelan protested as he realized that Harmonium was fixing to go with him.

"Nonsense, it's already been decided," the burly monk replied.

"And just who decided this?" Lazelan asked, throwing his hands in the air and knowing already that he might regret the answer.

"Bessie here," Harmonium answered matter-of-factly, gesturing to the brown horse with the white starburst on her face. He made ready to mount up.

"Wait, did you say Bessie?" Lazelan asked, dumbfounded. "Isn't that more of a name for a-"

"Now now, there's no need for name-calling. Bessie's very sensitive about things like that," Harmonium explained, "She's a fine beast, and a faster horse, you'll not find."

"But, *Bessie?*" Lazelan asked, "Why not something that sounds fast then, like speed or storm or something?"

"*I* didn't name her!" Harmonium replied indignantly, "that's what she told me her name was."

"You talk to horses now?" Lazelan asked incredulously.

"No," Harmonium replied simply, "but rangers do, and it was one of those that told me. Anyway, that's neither here nor there," he said as he swung himself up into the saddle. "What's in a name? Would a peony smell any less sweet if it were called a rock? Oh, I rather like that, someone should write that down one day."

Defeated, Lazelan led them toward the east, and they left the white stone house behind them.

Chapter 4
☼ Pest Control ☼

They decided to trek back through the city of Ethik on their way to the Embralic Desert. True, Lazelan had just come from there, but it was better than the alternative of travelling a farther distance in the wild or worse yet, through the scorching empty desert. At least this way they would be able to stay at an inn for the night instead of sleeping in the rough.

Lazelan lived in a borough where it was quiet and quaint, and full of friendly people always willing to lend a hand. After his time working as a palace mage, he was quite the celebrity there. Our travellers wanted to avoid notice and the obvious questions folk would ask if people thought they saw the mage returning. It was for this reason that they skirted those outlying homes, and decided to enter the city at the town gates.

Ethik was a bustling centre of activity, as it housed the university that people came to from around the world. Magic was not only believed in on this side of the world, but it was honored and treated as a privilege for those who could wield it. The stronger a person's abilities were, the more prestigious they were considered to be. Still, nobody ever dared look down on those who couldn't cast. Everyone had something they were good at, and you never knew if that something involved a sharp pointy object.

Because of the size of the city and the amount of strangers that came and went on any given day, there were town guards that were posted at all of the gates. The farm land, and the neighbours that knew Lazelan well, lived outside the gates and away from the hub-bub.

Harmonium and Lazelan dismounted from their horses, and approached one such gate as they travelled along the tall walls that surrounded the city. There were the sounds of a commotion up ahead, so they quickened their pace.

"I tell you, I know the man personally!" cried a smallish voice quite forcefully.

"Unless you can tell me what business you have with him, you're not getting in!" replied a gruff voice that could only belong to one of the guards.

"I told you already, I can't tell you, do you know how much trouble I would be in with him?" he bellowed indignantly, "The information is for his ears only! It wouldn't be secret if I told every guard at every town I travelled through to get here!"

It was at that point in the conversation that Lazelan and Harmonium rounded the corner and had the gates, guard, and what appeared at first to be a boy in armour, in sight.

Upon seeing the two mages, the guards straightened, having been bent over to confront the small person that stood no higher than three feet tall. Now that they had drawn nearer, Lazelan could see that it was in fact a full-grown man that rose only to the guard's belt. He had a full head of thick brown hair, and wore a hard leather breastplate, dyed green, with a picture of a hippogriff detailed in paint on the front. From his waist hung a long dagger, which seemed more like a short sword on the man. Harmonium advanced till he was almost between them.

"What seems to be the trouble here?" Harmonium asked jovially. The small man glared at the monk's back.

"This here *gentleman*," the guard sneered, "is claiming to be a personal friend of Harmonium Magster."

Lazelan looked from the guard to the dwarf, who showed no recognition of the man who stood before him. "I doubt that very much," Lazelan said plainly.

"Says you!" shot the man who stood to just under Lazelan's waist. "He and I go way back."

"Is that so?" Harmonium asked as he raised one wiry eyebrow. "Well, it just so happens that I can take you to meet him," he happily informed the diminutive man. Then to the town guard: "Let us pass, please." The guard jumped at this, and hesitated. "Don't worry," Harmonium assured him, "I'll take full responsibility for him until he has concluded his business in Ethik."

Satisfied with that, the guard stepped aside and allowed the three to pass through the city walls. Lazelan wasn't sure about this one. Harmonium had vouched for him, but the little man was clearly trouble if the guards were keeping him out, they let nearly everyone in. Now the little man was associated with the two mages though. Lazelan had worked hard to earn the sterling reputation he now enjoyed, and he wanted to keep it that way. He was going to stay alert around the child-sized traveller.

The small man paused, stood on tip toe, and began to shout at the guards in annoyance. "This is because I'm not as tall as you, isn't it? Oh sure, the little man can't possibly know such a one as Harmonium Magster, he's just a wee one of no consequence! Yet this here tall man comes along and says it's alright to let me in, and suddenly you're all rainbows, unicorns and sunshine. You know what I think?" The little man now bellowed, "I think your mother's a-"

With a quick wave of Lazelan's well-groomed hand, the little man continued to make a fuss, but the sound of his voice was instantly cut off. For a moment, the man continued to silently bellow before he realized that he was no longer making any noise.

"I'm sure your mother is a lovely woman," Lazelan assured the guard as Harmonium ushered the little warrior past the guards with a quiet warning in his ear.

"It is not wise to pester the town guards. They don't seem like much, but they can control whether or not you ever enter Ethik again. They can circulate your description to other town guards and make travelling very difficult for you." The man's face lost the redness it had gained in his angry verbal assault, and he nodded his understanding. Lazelan dropped his silencing spell.

Once inside, the short one prepared to make a quick departure. "Well, I thank you for your assistance, though I was really doing fine on my own," he thanked them grudgingly. "Now if you don't mind..." He let his voice trail off as he took a couple of tentative steps away from them.

"Not so fast! We told you we'd take you to meet the great Harmonium Magster, and that's exactly what we aim to do," Lazelan informed him. The man's shoulders slumped. "I really must decline, as we have business of the most secretive nature," the little man tried to convince them in a voice that let them know he was almost ready to accept defeat.

"Now, now, enough of this," Harmonium chided, "We should head somewhere for refreshments on the way, all this arguing makes me parched."

The little man brightened at this idea. "I know just the place!" he announced, seemingly in good spirits once again. "It's a little rough and tumble, but you lot seem like you can handle it. It might be a bit on the shady side, but it has great service, hearty meals, and because of the patronage, they don't get any of those university-types in there." Lazelan and Harmonium exchanged a glance before the man went on.   "One thing though, I would suggest that you bed down your horses at the common stables here in town.   If you tie them up outside the tavern, there's no guarantee that your mounts will still be there when we come out."

Chapter 5
☼ The Roughly Pitched Slug ☼

Lazelan had been in many a tavern through his travels in life, but none had prepared him for what he was faced with when the door swung open at the Roughly Pitched Slug.

Normally during the day, a tavern was quiet, as people generally saved their imbibing for the night time. The evenings were generally more lively. The air would be filled with the sound of loud conversation, boisterous laughter and sometimes the music or poetry of a bard or minstrel. Occasionally, a fight would break out in the wee hours of the morning due to a fool cheating at cards, but those instances were few and far between. Those that visited a tavern during the day would usually keep to themselves, finding some quiet solace in a flagon of ale.

These patrons, however, had it completely backward. As the three crossed the threshold, fists flew on the left and right. So many things had spilled and had been neglected over the years, that the various substances made Lazelan's sandals stick to the floor as they walked. It was disgusting. He didn't even want to think about what might be clinging to the bottom of his hand-crafted shoes.

Women that wore dresses that were far too revealing could be seen chatting or drinking with the men at various tables, and shady looking scoundrels held conferences with one another as they kept an untrusting hand on the hilt of their daggers. Money was changing hands where most of these conversations were taking place.

It was easy enough to miss the short man walking through the pub, but the two well-groomed mages stuck out like a sore thumb. Lazelan ducked into a nearby booth where they would attract less attention. Once the three were seated, they had to wait for a serving girl to come to the table. It took a while, and they began to get restless for their drinks. Finally, the little man reached out and snared the skirt of a wench bustling by with a tray of ale. She turned on the offender, and he quickly shot at her "Go on and send Tanina over now, would ya, love?"

The serving girl seemed to pull herself up a couple of inches, and freed her dress from his grasp with one hard yank that almost pulled him from his chair. "You!" she cried indignantly.

"Aye, now go get Tanina, wench, before I show you the backside of my sword," he agreed. As she hurried away, incensed, he called after her: "And send her with three suppers with stout mugs of ale."

Lazelan sat stunned at the mouth on this diminutive person. "Who *are* you?" he asked. He had been raised never to speak in such a way to a lady, then again, he had never been in the company of a lady such as these.

"I am no one of your concern," he answered haughtily. "I told you, I have important business with Harmonium Magster. You need not know anything else."

Lazelan leaned forward, ready to set the man straight, but Harmonium casually held up a hand to stop him. "Peace, Lazelan, the intrigue will unfold before too long."

"You sound like my friend Sasha," Lazelan grumbled, but spoke no more on the subject.

"Wait!" the man interjected, "Did he just call you Lazelan?" Lazelan nodded and the man hurriedly went on. "As in the king's mage? That Lazelan?"

"The former king's mage, but yes," Lazelan corrected him. The little man seemed to turn as white as a ghost. "I take it you have heard of me?" Lazelan asked with a chuckle.

"There isn't a gnome in the kingdom that hasn't heard of you!" The small man professed. *A gnome then*, Lazelan realized, *that explains a lot.* Lazelan had almost mistaken the man for a dwarf at first, but all of the dwarves Lazelan had met were stocky, and were tough as nails, with long beards and a certain gallantness that this gent surely lacked. He had only heard of gnomes before. They were also shorter than the average man, but they were more proportionate, and slighter of build like this fellow. They were supposed to be feisty care-free souls, and quite good-natured. This was the first time he had met one, and he wasn't sure how he stacked up against others of his kind.

The gnome started to nod slowly to himself as if speedily thinking something through. His nodding quickened, "I think you may be of some service then," he informed the mage hastily, as a giant man in a shirt and a dirty white apron pushed people out of his way. He was making a b-line from the bar to their table.

The little man licked his lips and begged in rushed voice. "Please, help me if you can, I can't leave here without speaking with Tanina!"

"I take it that's not Tanina then," Lazelan jested, and cocked a thumb to indicate the cook that was closing the gap between his ample belly and the table at which the adventurers sat. The small man was so agitated that he offered no snide remark, only shook his head in answer. Lazelan looked to Harmonium, who nodded back, *Sure, you take this one.*

The huge man with the dirty white apron and impressively muscled arms pushed the last people out of his way and arrived at the table, bumping into it roughly. "You," he indicated the little man with a meaty finger pointed in his face," are not welcome here. Out the lot of you, we don't cater to no riff-raff as the likes of him, or his friends!"

"Whatever he has done in the past," Lazelan answered amicably, "I can swear that he will do nothing to wrong you this evening. Besides, this is the honorable Harmonium Magster, and I'm sure you would appreciate his custom."

The gnome jumped as if stung on the rump by a bee. The large bartender looked unsure, switching his gaze from the little man he did not want there, to the well-known mage his business could benefit from. Finally, he agreed to let them stay when Lazelan produced a silver coin and slid it across the table for his inconvenience.

The burly man returned to his post behind the bar, leaving the gnome sitting for the moment speechless beside the two very magical men.

"Now that my secret is out," said Harmonium, "perhaps you could explain to me what our very important business is about."

"Ah...um...well, you see...we actually don't have any," the gnome reluctantly admitted, "I've never actually met you before."

"It would have been news to me if you had," Lazelan responded automatically, but Harmonium raised two fingers to silence him.

"I have spent a lifetime building a good name for myself, I value my reputation greatly," Harmonium informed him. "I would be very...shall we say *upset* if my name were drawn into a dishonest scheme," the monk warned.

Chapter 6
✿   All Bets Are On   ✿

"Look, I just had to get to this tavern," the man insisted nervously. "I used to work for Andreus, that's Andy over there," he motioned to the huge man in the apron behind the bar. "He doesn't want me here because I raised a fuss about being cheated out of my rightfully earned money. My name is Wolfbane Willowswitch, ask anyone, they'll know who I am. I supplied the tavern here with meat for their menu. I would hunt it and bring it here in exchange for coin. The bigger the game, the more payout Andy would give me.

A few weeks back, Andy was preparing to have a big name come to the tavern to perform. The talk around town led him to believe that the crowd here would be enormous. He asked me to bring in larger game than I was used to in order to feed all the guests. So, I went out into the wilderness. I was lucky enough to track and bring down a dire elk. I returned with it, but when I arrived, Andreus wouldn't pay," he said grimly. "Apparently, the talents of the travelling bard had been greatly exaggerated, and during his warm up performance in the afternoon, he had actually been booed off the platform. Andy said that so much meat would be a burden for him to sell because now he expected a much smaller crowd. Andy took my elk and offered me my regular fee for a brace of rabbits," Wolfbane informed them.

As he spun his tale, another serving girl came to the table with a tray full of plates and mugs. This girl was far from pretty, with mousy brown ringlets that fell past her shoulders. Her hair was dull and tousled, and her bodice was laced wrong where the chord missed some of the eyelets. She had dark bags under her eyes which made her look as if she hadn't slept in a month, and when she smiled in greeting, Lazelan could see that half of her teeth were either missing or rotted down to black stumps. Wolfbane greeted her with "Ah, and here's Tanina!" but she only nodded and didn't interrupt their conversation as she laid the food on the table.

"What did you do?" Lazelan asked the gnome and noticed that the new serving girl lingered by the table side.

"Well, I had done my work, and I was determined to get paid my rightful share. I waited until that night, and returned to the bar, this time as a paying customer. I circulated around the tavern, chatting up the people at the other tables. Eventually I made my way to the bar itself where Andy was working serving up the orders. I challenged him to a bet. He was famous for making wagers with out-of-towners that they couldn't possibly win.

"Why would they take the bet then?" Harmonium inquired.

"It wasn't obvious that they would lose," Wolfbane told them. "He had a scam you see, he would use the same one every time. He would bet them that they couldn't finish a platter of quail and a mug of ale before him. He had only one rule: neither person could lay a finger on the other person's food or dishes. Then he would set up a platter for each of them, a bone bowl, and a drink. Someone would shout "go", and then the stranger would start chowing down. Andy would simply take his bone bowl, and turn it upside down over their ale."

"He effectively ends the bet because the other person can't get to their drink to finish his end of the bargain," Lazelan realized aloud.

"Yeah," Wolfbane continued, "and he hadn't technically cheated because he didn't touch their food or plates directly, only his own bone bowl.

"What was stopping the opponent from putting their own bowl over his drink?" Harmonium inquired.

Wolfbane shrugged, but the quiet lass by the table side piped up: "I only saw it once, when he bet a man from Ebonyshire, but Andy was ready for that too. He kept his own mug of ale on the very edge of the bar, so almost half was overhanging the edge of the wood, you see.

When he placed his bowl over the guest's drink, the man picked up his own bowl and covered Andy's. Andy simply reached up under the bowl from below the bar where the mug was overhanging. He was able to pick up his mug no problem, then used the edge of the bar to tip off the other man's bowl," she finished.

"So I assume you found another way to beat him?" Lazelan asked Wolfbane.

"No, I lost the bet with Andy, but I still bested him," the gnome informed them with a twinkle in his eye. I pretended that I was in on his scheme and that I had figured a way to beat him. He couldn't resist the bet. I told him that I wanted to change the set-up of things to up the stakes. There was to be only one bone bowl for us to share, and I told him that I wanted more than just one quail, boasting that I could out eat him any day. That fairly made him laugh out loud due to my stature, you see.

He ordered a meal of each kind be brought to the bar top. There was stew, pork, and part of my elk as well as the quail all laid out on the bar. The smells made my already nervous stomach twist, and as someone yelled "Go," I made a half-hearted attempt to reach the bowl before he did. Of course I let him win and watched expectantly as he turned the only bone bowl over my mug of ale.

"Then you had lost," Harmonium pointed out.

"Yes, in a manner of speaking," Wolfbane admitted, "But that wasn't the end of it. Andy stood there chuckling as I began to tear into the meat. I pointed out that if he didn't eat too, he won't have truly won the bet. I reminded him that the terms were that he finish everything before me. If he didn't finish it, I wasn't going to pay him. I told him that I was still planning on eating more than him and finishing all of it to boot! That's when he finally looked a little worried and picked up the first bit of food.

"So there was no winner," Lazelan concluded, "There was so much food that neither of you could finish. Now the mage thought he understood why Andreus didn't want the gnome around. He had outsmarted the barkeep at his own game.

"Actually, Andy did win the bet. By the end of it more than half of my food and all of his was gone. We had both slowed down, with bulging fat bellies, both of us unsure as to if we could eat even one more bite. But he managed. Triumphantly, he picked up his mug of ale and drank it down in small slurps. I paid him the 20 silver I had bet him, and he laughed and shook my hand."

Confused, Lazelan asked "So why is it that you're not welcome here, and what money are you seeking?"

"Well, after the bet was through and Andy was paid, I circulated the bar collecting money I was owed by the other patrons. Andy saw this and called me out. I informed him that I had lost my bet with him, but that was ok. At the same time, I had bet everyone else there that by the end of the night we would have littered his bar, and that not only would he be ok it, he would have helped! Andy looked down to regard the bones, grease and carcasses left on the bar top. Most of the mess from their eating had not stayed on the plates, and seeing as how the only bone bowl was still turned down over my drink, we had simply chucked the bones aside as we devoured the food."

Harmonium and Lazelan began to laugh, but low, so as not to draw notice from the large man behind the bar. "Very smart, my little friend," Harmonium congratulated him.

"Yes, but he was offended. He said I took advantage of him and swiped my full purse of coins. He said he was going to use it because he was going to have to pay the serving girls overtime to clean up the mess I had caused."

"He never paid us though, he just kept it," the unfortunate girl piped up.

"Thank you, Tanina," the gnome replied, "That is one of the things I had come to find out. I don't want anyone to lose out because of my stunt. I have come to collect my rightful money back; I won it fair and square. I see it as what I should have justly gotten for my elk. It could have fed a village for a week, or me for over a month."

Chapter 7
✪ Turning the Tables ✪

     The three sat at the table eating and drinking, while Tanina retired to tend to the other tables in the bar. They tried to come up with a way to get back the gnome's money without causing a scene. Lazelan was looking forward to this. He loved a good challenge, and he could feel the cogs begin to turn in his mind. He put another bite of food into his mouth and chewed thoughtfully as he tried to find a way around the problem. The food was alright, but it was hard to enjoy a meal cooked by someone who had wronged one of their members.

     Wolfbane suggested using magic to draw the coins to them, but Lazelan and Harmonium wouldn't hear of it.

     "It's not about what we are able or unable to do," Lazelan explained to their downcast companion, "it's that whether we would be in the right or not, it would make us no better than petty criminals. We are not thieves, but we will find a way," the mage assured him.

     They were about halfway through their mugs of ale when their opportunity arose. With a loud *bang*, the door slammed opened all the way to the wall with such force that a cloud of dust was produced from the dirt between the boards when it hit. If that hadn't been enough, the sheer size of the man that entered silenced the rest of the revellers. He was easily seven and a half feet tall, and so wide that he had to duck and turn slightly sideways to get in through the door.

     "I bet he has muscles on top of muscles," Wolfbane intoned in awe. Intrigued, Lazelan put down the piece of meat he was eating, and cleaned the grease from his fingers as he watched the scene before him unfold.

The man looked absolutely barbaric, wearing nothing but a heavy furry pelt around his middle and large mud-stained boots that rose halfway up his calves. His skin had an undeniable greenish tinge, and two thick canine teeth poked up and out of his mouth from his bottom jaw like those of a boar.

A half-orc, Lazelan realized from his teachings, born of one human parent and one beastly green orc. *I wonder why he's so far south from his clan.*

The creature carried a huge axe in one hand, and had a large crossbow strapped across his back. A quiver of bolts hung from the belt that appeared to hold his fur clothing together. He addressed the room in the common tongue, but his broken sentences and thick accent pegged him as someone who could understand a lot more of a language than he could speak. Still, it was clear that he knew enough to get his message across.

"Where is this Andreus, I would make bet with him," the man bellowed in a thunderously deep voice. To Lazelan, the words sounded distorted with his heavy accent, so it came out sounding like *"Vere is dis Andreus, I vould make bet vit him."*

Somewhere in the tavern, someone dropped their cutlery and there was a distinct *ting, ting, ting, tink* in the otherwise silent room as it clattered to the floor. The fat bartender, who had been wiping down the bar with large swipes of his rag, seemed to have found one place in particular very dirty, as he kept circling around and around the same spot. Perhaps he thought that if he stared at the spot hard enough, it would remove itself.

Eventually, someone raised a shaking hand, and pointed toward the bar. The large hulking figure moved through the tavern with long strides of his muscled legs. He stopped in front of Andreus, who finally looked up.

It looked to Lazelan like the bartender was having a hard time meeting the fellow's eyes.

"I've never seen old Andy look scared before," Wolfbane whispered.

"I'll bet he's not used to seeing many men larger than he," Harmonium reasoned, "Let's see how this pans out."

The half-orc said: "You will get the foods and drink now."

"Oh, I never bet out of principle," Andy lied unconvincingly.

The large greenish man began to unstrap his crossbow from his back with solemn eyes. Andy began to panic.

"Anyhow, I'm not in much of a betting mood tonight," the bartender driveled.

Lazelan began to get nervous as the beastly man started to load a bolt into the cross bow. He looked at Harmonium for a clue as to how long he was going to let this go before they would interfere. He had no love for the cheating bartender, but neither did he like bloodshed if it could be avoided. Harmonium seemed to be studying the half-orc like a specimen back at the university.

With the loaded crossbow now at the ready, the half-orc tried one last time. "You were willing to bet my brother, and you cheat him. Now, you will bet with me, and no cheat."

Andreus gulped and began to set drinks on the bar with visibly shaking hands. He whispered hoarsely to one of the serving girls who began to bring the plates of food. Lazelan's stomach sank as Andy looked over at Wolfbane at their table, but the bartender only said "Not on the bar, though, we need to find a table."

With those words, a foursome of grim looking fellows cleared out from the table closest the bar, saying: "Here Andy, you can use ours." Andy only nodded weakly and began to transfer the food. Finally the men were sitting face to face with each other, the large green man's gaze boring into the eyes of his opponent. "Go."

At first neither of them moved. Andy's hand twitched as he looked down to the bone bowl. Lazelan could hear the guttural growl that erupted deep down in the beastly man's throat. The bartender decided it was a better idea to start eating instead.

It was over in minutes. Lazelan had never seen a half-orc at work on a meal before but it was the stuff that legends are made of. The man had simply picked up his plate, tilted his head back, and tipped the whole contents of his serving down his gullet. With some gnashing of his giant teeth, he ate the quail, bones and all. He finished his ale in the same manner, and slammed his tankard down on the table with one hand, while wiping his forearm across his mouth with the other.

"I win," he pointed out.

Andy sat in shock with the first quail wing still dangling from his greasy fingers. It fell unceremoniously back onto his heaping plate.

"But that's not fair-" he managed to utter before the beast rose up before him, grabbed for his cross-bow with one hand and flipped the table between them out of the way with the other.

Chapter 8
☼ Hang-Ups ☼

"This has just gotten interesting," Harmonium announced.

"What, just now?" Wolfbane asked incredulously, "What about all that other stuff? You know, the whole unhinging his jaw like a snake! Well I'll bet he could eat a gnome whole!" he jested.

"Indeed," Harmonium agreed without any hint of a smile. The gnome gulped. But Lazelan had caught the wink thrown at him by his old teacher. *Still*, the young mage thought, *the half-orc would be a formidable opponent*.

"It's almost time," Harmonium shared.

"Woah, wait a minute," the gnome protested, "you're not actually going to suggest that we get involved, are you?"

"Do you want your money back or not?" Lazelan asked.

"Well yes," Wolfbane admitted, "But I'd also like to keep both my arms so I can hold it, and count it, and generally admire the small mound sitting in my hands!"

Lazelan smiled, he had to admit that the gnome had a way of putting things that was quite entertaining. Perhaps they should keep him around a while longer. He focused his attention back on the bartender and his guest.

"You will pay me now, the coins for this bet you lost, and the monies you stole from my brother," the half-orc said grimly. His thick accent making it sound to Lazelan like *"You vill pay me now, de coins for dis bet you lost, and de monies you stole from me bruder."*

"But that's not fair," the bartender was able

to repeat before everything seemed to move in slow motion.

The half-orc's fingers squeezed, unleashing the cross-bow's bolt, and Lazelan threw out a hand toward the scared bartender who had screwed his eyes shut in preparation for the impact.

Andreus was suddenly swept upward still holding onto his seat, and was suspended above the on-looking crowd. Harmonium stood and swept an arm back, causing a metal serving tray to fly out of a serving wench's hands and flash through the air. There was a hollow *clang* as the crossbow bolt hit the makeshift shield just inches from another patron's head.

"Eek!" the guest exclaimed, and promptly ran for the door.

"I could be wrong," Wolfbane mused, "but I think old Andy might have just lost himself a customer."

The half-orc, realizing with a blink that his shot had missed, pulled out a new bolt to reload.

"Let's not be so hasty, my good er...man," Wolfbane addressed the beast, raising his voice and climbing up on the table to be seen.

The green giant turned to the sound of the voice, but didn't stop reloading his weapon. Wolfbane climbed upon the table so he could speak to the creature face-to-face. He was disturbed to realize that he still only came to the beast's armpit.

"You see, he owes me money too, and if you kill him, I won't see a penny of it either."

Even from his precarious place, Andy still growled "I don't owe nobody nothing, I won that fair and..." he let his voice trail off with the withering look he was getting from both the half-orc and the gnome.

Wolfbane hopped down from the table and

walked over to where Andy was suspended, looking up at him, he said: "As far as I can tell, my friends over there just saved your life, so right now you owe me a great deal more than what you stole from me."

Andy stewed quietly. "This is what I'm proposing," Wolfbane went on, "You give this here guest whatever you owe him, for the bet you clearly just lost, and for his brother. Then you'll go in the back and get the purse you took from me. In exchange, we'll make sure that when we all leave you here, you'll still be alive and well." He looked to the half-orc to see if he would ascent to that, and he nodded his agreement.

"Or," Wolfbane continued, "we could simply leave you there. He seems to be a pretty good shot," he added, motioning to the tray containing the last crossbow bolt. He and the two mages stood and made ready to leave.

"Fine," Andreus hastily agreed, but the men continued to gather their things.

"I said *fine*, I'll pay back the money, just get me down from here!" the suspended bartender implored them.

Lazelan lowered Andreus to the floor, and he turned toward the bar. "It's back there," he told them, and indicated the back room.

"I'll just go around back," Harmonium told Lazelan in a low voice, "in case our *friend* tries to slip out unnoticed." Lazelan nodded that he understood, and walked the bartender as far as the bar. Harmonium left through the door they had come in through, but not before leaving money on the table for their meals. Lazelan watched as Tanina made the money disappear into a pocket in her apron. He wondered if old Andy would ever see that money.

Andreus disappeared into the back room and

as the minutes ticked by, Lazelan grew tenser. He listened hard for noise of a skirmish happening outside, but it was difficult to hear anything over the din of patrons eating and talking that had returned to the bar.

The bartender finally returned with a fat purse in one hand. In the other, he held a small stack of silver and copper coins. These he handed to the half-orc, and the purse he handed to the gnome. Wolfbane couldn't hold it in one hand, and had to use two to accept the bulging leather that contained what must have been a small fortune.

With his money counted and pocketed, the half-orc left Andreus with a warning not to try to cheat anyone from Ebonyshire again.

As the door closed behind him, Wolfbane palmed his face with a loud *smack*. "Of course, Ebonyshire, I thought I recognized his brand of ugly," he commented.

"Ebonyshire?" Lazelan asked.

"Yes," Harmonium replied, "one of two villages nestled in the Evenwood forest."

"But I thought that that forest was uninhabitable," Lazelan put forth.

"Yeah, to you or me maybe," the gnome replied, "but anyone who hit that many branches on their fall down the ugly tree would be just fine. It's all full of mutants and weird creatures. Nothing palatable will grow there, people have tried. A really creepy place if you ask me."

"Don't judge the man too harshly," Harmonium reprimanded him, "He was acting nobly on the behalf of his brother after all."

"I agree," Lazelan admitted, "It must have taken a great amount of courage to travel to a place so different from his own looking the way he does. I can only imagine the danger he is putting himself in, knowing how men act out of fear of things that are different or unknown."

"Alright, alright," Wolfbane surrendered, chastised. "He's very brave and I shouldn't mock him. I will think next time before I speak." He subconsciously fondled the leather purse of winnings from the tavern.

"How much did you end up gaining?" Lazelan asked out of curiosity. He knew the bet he had lost was sizable, twenty silver was enough to pay for a fortnight at a nice inn, with meals included.

"I wagered a gold coin to anyone who wanted to take up the bet," Wolfbane replied proudly.

Lazelan whistled. If even two people had wagered against him, he would have broken even for the silver he had lost to Andreus. "So how many people paid up?" he inquired. A huge grin spread across the gnome's face.

"Thirty-five," he replied proudly. Lazelan was dumbfounded. *Now there was more than a bit of cunning,* he thought in his shock. *We could use that. We could use all the help we can get, really.* He looked to Harmonium for the go-ahead before asking the gnome:

"Do you by any chance like adventure as much as you like gold?"

The little man seemed to size both of them up. He shrugged noncommittally, and started heading in the direction of the stables.

"Just out of curiosity, what would you have done if Andreus hadn't offered to return your winnings?" Lazelan asked, starting after him. He was determined to get an answer, and wanted to keep the man talking.

"I would have left him there," Wolfbane responded immediately.

"What, up in the air? Don't you think that

would have been a bit awkward?" Lazelan pressed.

"Old Andy always did just seem to hang around the place," he responded with a pun.

"That's terrible," Lazelan admonished while shaking his head at the horrible joke.

"Well honestly, if he's going to cheat people, he can't get hung up on someone wanting their money back," Wolfbane continued.

Lazelan just looked at him, without laughing. "I think I'm beginning to reconsider."

"That's my sense of humour, and it's coming with us," The gnome replied.

Chapter 9
✿ A World Away ✿

In a dusky room in Elbon, a boy of eleven cleared the dishes from in front of a knight and his lady at the supper table. His sure fingers moved the knives and spoons, along with the tankard and flagon, to a tray that would help him carry the load to the kitchen all at once. He was happy in his duties, and was proud of the fact that his wealthy family had found him this job with his uncle and aunt. He had served as a page boy for House Sprig for almost four years. One day, if he kept working hard, they had assured him he would become a squire, and would move from the service of Lady Elewys, to serve Sir Stanton. Under the knight, he would learn the skills necessary to eventually become knighted himself.

So far, he had excelled in learning respect and propriety while completing any given task, and his aunt Elewys had often complimented him as being the most polite of all the pages that served her. Stanton stood and walked over to the hearth where the light was stronger from the fire.

"Will there be anything else, my lord, my la-*dy*?" the boy's voice cracked embarrassingly as he addressed the couple. Cal clapped a hand over his mouth, and Lady Elewys looked down, concealing a smile. The knight's head shot up, and he caught Calen's eye before exchanging a meaningful look with his wife.

Stanton had drawn his sword, and had been examining it for nicks or dullness of the blade. He never brought it to the table at meals, and the boy thought that was probably a good rule. The child rarely got to see it up close, however, as he was always busy running messages or doing other work that kept him in the lady's service at the manor house. *One day,* he often thought with excitement, *perhaps I'll get to actually hold it.* Perhaps that day was now closer that he thought.

"No thank you, Calen, that will be all," the knight replied kindly, then after another glance at his wife, and her approving nod, he seemed to change his mind. "Actually Cal, come here," he ordered. Before sending him off, Stanton put a hand on Cal's shoulder and told him, "I know you have only been my wife's page for four years, however, the change is coming upon you. You will travel with us to Endalwynndale on the morrow, and will begin being educated in the practices of a squire. There will be much to learn. I ask that you do your best, as you have always done for my Elewys, and if you do, you should be fine. Life as a squire is much more difficult and can be hard on a boy, but we will see how you manage."

Cal looked nervously to Lady Elewys, who had always been so kind to him. She nodded again reassuringly. *I am going to miss her,* he realized, but this is what he had been training for, and his heart elated at the news. "Thank you, sir." he replied emphatically.

"Now, off with you to bed," Stanton said, dismissing him. The page bowed politely and began to move to exit the room. "Oh, and Cal," Stanton got the boy's attention before the door snicked shut behind him, "Rest up tonight, we will have a busy day tomorrow."

Cal let the door close and began his trek downstairs toward the kitchen. Every day was a busy day, but he knew that the knight meant that the next day would the the first in his new role, filled with a multitude of new tasks to master. The tell-tale crack of his voice had been the end of his service under Lady Elewys. Sir Stanton was leaving on the morrow to begin a journey to the beautiful castle in Endalwynndale. It looked as though Cal had gotten himself invited to go along. His heart soared. He hoped he was ready. This change was coming upon him earlier than with some of the other boys that had become squires, so he would have to work all the harder to measure up. True, he wouldn't be an adept squire yet, but this would be the beginning!

In a few short days, upon arriving at the castle, the knight would show Cal how to dress him for battle. Cal would have to learn how the armour fit together and in which order to put the pieces on. It was a big step for him, and he knew that if he did a good job, the next task would be for him to learn how to clean the knight's weapons. His rise of exuberance was quashed by a stab of fear.

Please, please, please, by all that is bright, let things go the way they're supposed to! he prayed. Lately, strange things had been happening. Things were beginning to just go wrong. He would set to a task with the full intent of doing his best at it; "Any job worth doing is worth doing well," his grandmother was fond of saying, and he fully believed that too. Especially when these jobs would one day lead him to his dream of gallantly fighting battles on horseback, saving ladies in distress, or perhaps winning tournaments as a full-fledged knight.

But he had been finding himself sluggish as of late. He went to bed at a good time, and rose when he should, but felt as though he hadn't slept a wink. He found it difficult to complete tasks that he would normally find easy just because he was so tired. He got frustrated at whatever he was trying to accomplish, and at himself for failing.

As each night passed, he found himself more and more fatigued, and today it had finally caught up with him. Partway through his task of laundering the clothing in the river, his eyes had drooped lower and lower, till they had shut completely. He had slumped forward in the water, and had gone under. He had woken with a start, but was tangled in the cloth which prevented him from swimming to save himself. Two washer wenches had to pull him free, sputtering and coughing and half drown.

After that, the knight had had the boy working within the manor walls to keep a closer eye on him. There hadn't been any more incidents of randomly falling asleep, but Cal dreaded what might happen the next day.

He finished off his chores and retired to eat his supper in the kitchen with the other servants. He liked eating there, it was when he was allowed to relax and share in good conversation. Everyone had leaned in across the wooden table, and were talking in hushed tones. They were discussing a rumour one of them had heard in the market.

"But didn't she hear anything?" one of the women at the table asked.

"No," one of the men responded, "she was fast asleep, never even stirred."

"Curious," one of the younger maids commented, "that all her other riches were just sitting there, and they didn't touch a thing."

The man-servant grunted reservedly, it wasn't his business, and he didn't want to speculate. He hated gossip.

"What has happened?" Cal asked as he placed his wooden bowl on the table and folded himself onto a space made for him on the bench.

"Lady Danelyn's signet ring was taken from her in the night, right out of her box of jewels beside where she was sleeping!" the maid reported. "But what of you?" she asked, "I heard you are rather tired of doing the lord's washing." She smirked at her clever joke.

"I don't understand it myself," he admitted, "I just feel so exhausted all the time."

"I'll send for Master Zalice again," the man-servant informed him.

"I've seen him three times this week," Calen protested, "and it doesn't seem to be helping."

"Nonsense child," the man-servant bristled, "respect your elders, they have seen a lot more of life than you. You said that you've been sleeping through the night, therefore, his potions must be working."

"Yes, sir," Cal grumbled almost under his breath.

"That's better," the man-servant acknowledged, "Now let us finish our meals in peace."

The servants of the knight's manor drained their bowls in silence one by one, leaving the table as they did. Eventually Calen finished and excused himself to await Master Zalice in the tiny room that had been afforded him. He removed his clothing from the day and dressed for a night of slumber, finishing by washing his hands and face in the basin in the corner. Other than his bed and chest, it was the only furniture in the room, but this did not bother him. He was here for the experience after all, he could rest in comfort when he became a knight and had a manor of his own.

He climbed into bed and thought of the exciting day ahead. He was wired. His head was full of thoughts and he realized there would be no sleep for him in the near future. He just wasn't tired. Perhaps it was a good idea they had called

Master Zalice for him after all.   It was then that he heard shuffling steps in the hall outside his room.

Chapter 10
✿ Turning the Page ✿

Zilla and Augden Zalice made a perfect pair. Zilla was a gardener and Augden a herbologist. He had originally started the endeavour as a hobby, but the folk that lived around him had found him to be quite skilled. His reputation had spread, and now some of the bigger manor houses and surrounding villages called on him when they needed medicines for various ailments.

He had met Zilla when he had run out of an herb he needed for a potion, and had ventured to see if he could borrow some. She had obliged, and over time they had pooled their resources to make a successful business and marriage. She was a good wife, and he a happy man, but he wanted more. He had hoped to one day serve the palace itself, but Prince Oslan's new wife was said to be a talented herbologist herself, and was even more skilled in casting magic. He just couldn't compete with that. He thought that perhaps when she was slowed with child he would get his chance if the nobles would put in a good word for him. Knights were always a good bet, they were often getting hurt on the battle field or earning bruises during practice. He had poultices that would help with those, and even broken bones. For now though, he would have to be content with the families he already served.

His wife knew he was dissatisfied, and had suggested talking to the lords and ladies of the court to pass on to their acquaintances word of his talents. He knew she was glad he served only a few. The bigger the area he served, the more time he would have to spend travelling away from her. She liked the fact that he was ambitious, but he was aware that she hated nights like these when he was called away from their warm bed for work.

The middle-aged man shuffled down the hall to the boy's room, his walking stick clicking at every couple of steps. His keen ears heard each *click, click* of the stick hitting the stone floor, as a rock tumbling down a mountainside. He was usually able-bodied, but he had taken a fall and had badly hurt his leg, making it increasingly difficult to get around. He found that the staff helped, and truth be told, he felt that it made him look rather distinguished. He had straight brown hair that was starting to grey at the temples, and was one of the lucky few that possessed a pair of spectacles. They were a new invention, and the fact that he could read again made a huge difference in his life of creating and scribing herbal remedies.

Knocking softly to announce his arrival, Master Zalice entered the boy's room with a warm smile.

"Good evening, Calen," he greeted the boy, "Trouble sleeping again?"

"Yes, Master Zalice," The boy admitted grudgingly. Cal had wanted to sleep well tonight, but had found himself filled with energy instead. If left to his own devices, he wasn't sure he would have been able to sleep at all because of the excitement of the next day. His worries and wonders about what tomorrow would bring kept circling in his mind like spiced wine being swirled in a goblet.

"Well no matter," the herbologist tried to comfort him, "we'll have you off to sleep in no time." He unshouldered his satchel and sat at the foot of the boy's narrow bed. He pulled from his bag a bottle containing a deep purple liquid, and unstopped the cork. Handing the mixture to the boy, he retrieved a silver coin from the pouch at his waist. Calen sat holding the mixture, but did not drink it. Used to dealing with the children of rich lords, the herbologist took his slowness to drink it in stride. "Pinch your nose, you won't be able to taste it," he suggested, "Well, not much," he shrugged apologetically.

Calen gulped, took in a big breath, pinched his nose and upended the contents of the round bottle into his mouth. He swallowed hard. Master Zalice watched as the boy released his nose and grimaced, sticking out his tongue and screwing up both eyes. The potion bore the sickly taste of berries that had sat ripening beyond the point where they were still good, fermenting and drawing fruit flies while mold clung to the outer edges. The child handed him back the empty bottle with a weak "Thanks".

The herbologist accepted the container, making it disappear back into his sac, and he gently laid the boy back onto his pillow.

"Now watch here," he instructed while showing the boy his silver coin. The boy's eyes followed it's movements as the flash of silver began to dance across the man's knuckles. It rolled over the back of Master Zalice's index finger, and as it came to sit upright in the crevice between it and the next, his finger lifted, and the next one dipped, sending it rolling over the middle finger. The boy watched, mesmerized as the coin travelled in a steady rhythm back and forth, back and forth across the backs of the sure digits.

The first time Cal had seen this, he had been amazed. The herbologist was quite practiced at it and Cal had never seen the coin falter. He listened to his visitor's voice and felt his eyes starting to burn with weariness. He resisted the urge to rub them. The boy's eyelids grew heavy and began to droop.

Master Zalice continued to make the coin flip over the backs of his knuckles.

"That's it," he coaxed the boy, "let the tiredness take you, feel free to sleep now." After a few more passes of the coin, Calen's eyes finally slid shut.

*　　　*　　　*

Hands clutched dark material in the light of a full moon. Yanking it aside revealed a chest of drawers behind the curtains. Atop the chest sat an ornate wooden box. The craftsmanship of that alone made it a valuable enough item, but that was not the object of this trip. The jewelry would be inside. Lifting a latch with a finger, the figure lifted the hinged lid to expose all manner of necklaces, trinkets and broaches. A ring was removed from the box, and cast aside. The other jewels clinked gently as it fell in amongst the bracelets. The burglar paused as the lord's steady snore was interrupted. The large form in the bed beside the chest of drawers moved under the covers, muttering to himself. The intruder held their breath, frozen, dark clothes blending into the shadows of the room. The snoring resumed, and so did the figure in black.

Ring after ring was checked before the villain finally found their prize. The rings bearing the lord's and lady's seals were silently set aside. The figure opened the flap of a pouch of their own, black like their outfit. From it, they drew out another equally ornate box. This one had rubies and emeralds on the top, and was opened to reveal a thick paper, sealing wax, and some matches.

The figure turned their back to the bed to shade the glow of the match from the sleeping forms under the canopy. The form spread out the folded paper and struck a match on the rough underside of the wood box. They held the red wax over the match's flame for a few seconds, and let it drip near the bottom of the document. Once two red blobs adorned the sheet, the figure blew out the match and pressed the two signet rings to the page. The acrid smell of the smoke in the air from the chemicals on the match caused the lord's snoring to once again stop as he began to cough drowsily. The person in black hastily packed up and dropped the jeweled box back into into the black leather pouch, and then made their way out the window to the ground below.

A guard doing his rounds heard the noise of booted feet scrabbling against stone. Following the sound, the guardsman saw the figure leap from the building to the ground, rolling to absorb the impact and coming to a stop back on their feet. The guard moved as he watched the figure in black pelt across the lawn and scramble up on top of the stone wall that surrounded the estate.

"Halt!" he cried loudly. But the figure only bowed low at the waist and crouched as if to give the guard a hand up. Moments before the guard got there, with sword drawn and bellowing in a voice to raise the alarm, the figure on the wall threw both hands heavenward and sprung up. The silhouette turned over once in the air in a neatly executed backflip. The guard watched helplessly as the intruder landed on the ground outside the gates, and ran off into the night to their lair, castle, or hovel.

Chapter 11
☼ A Heated Discussion ☼

Lazelan was beginning to consider that this might have been a rash decision. The gnome, cheerful enough as he was, had not halted his talking in almost three hours of travel. *Doesn't he have to stop to breathe?* Lazelan wondered tiredly.

"So I say: what's a lizard doing on his face anyway? Well, I swear to you, it was at that very moment..."

Lazelan tuned out Wolfbane's prattle, and focussed on his surroundings. The three sat atop their mounts, travelling at a fast walk. They had abandoned the road and had begun crossing the plains between Ethik and the Embralic Desert. The rich ferns and lush green ground-cover this half of the world was known for had begun to thin. The plants grew more and more sparse and more stick-like. Here and there a cactus began to show with their spikes poking out of their smooth green skin. As they grew closer to the desert, the loose soil gave way to packed dirt that began to look dry and cracked like leather that had not been oiled in years.

There was a flash of darkness as a great shadow rolled over them, momentarily blotting out the sun the way a shark does to the sea creatures below. Lazelan caught the quick movement in his peripheral vision and looked to the sky, his breath catching in his throat. He saw sand-coloured fur, great wings, and a tufted tail as the creature soared away in the same direction they were heading.

Lazelan had instinctively sought the electric ball of blazing energy at his core. This was the powerful orb all mages harnessed and manipulated with Almatrae, the ancient language of magic, to create their feats. Combined with the right incantations, it could be sent from the mage to do endless wondrous acts of good or evil. New mages had to first learn to find their energy, and often had to say the words aloud, but he had practiced over years, and using magic to do his bidding came now as second nature to him. He released the channelled energy now, seeing that they were in no immediate danger.

"Well, *that* doesn't bode well," Wolfbane offered, "Perhaps we should make camp here, you know, let it get a little farther ahead."

"Not a bad idea," Harmonium agreed, much to Lazelan's surprise. "The sun is at its peak, and the sand is only going to serve to reflect the heat of its rays. From here on in, we would be wise to rest during the sweltering light of day, and resume our travels in the cool breezes of the night." As if to accentuate his point, a bead of sweat rolled down the side of his face, and he wiped it away with a bland orangey-red cloth. As if in turn, Lazelan became more aware of sweat trailing down his own face, and began to rummage in his pack.

Evidently, Wolfbane took this as a sign. "Great, I was beginning to think we'd never stop for lunch. Which of us is going to set up the tent? I'm not quite tall as the tent poles, so perhaps I should do what I do best and supervise."

Lazelan eyed the older man, this was a test, he was sure of it. "No, I don't think so," he decided. He removed a long rectangle of light coloured cloth from his satchel. He tied it to cover his head of thick red curls. It helped, a bit. The sun didn't seem to press down on him so forcefully.

"What?" the gnome objected, "But I thought the *master* over here just said-"

"What he says and what he means is not always the same thing," Lazelan answered simply.

"True enough it is hot during the day, but at night the desert plummets to cold temperatures. We are dressed for day, with loose flowing clothes. If we were to try to travel at night dressed like this, we'd freeze. You have your leather armour strapped to your horse, but we do not. We will need the shelter of the tent and the warmth of our bedrolls to survive the desert nights," he finished.

Harmonium looked at him and only nodded. Lazelan was filled with pride. From his old master, this was as close to a clap on the back as one got.

Wolfbane started muttering, looking longingly back at his leathers, "What's the point of armour if you can't even wear it?" he asked mournfully, thinking of the sweltering heat.

"Tell you what," Harmonium allowed, "you can take late night watch."

"Well that's just great!" Wolfbane mumbled, being smart enough for once to keep his grumblings to himself.

"What was that?" Lazelan jibed.

"I was just saying that I'm glad he's your teacher and not mine," the gnome announced.

Lazelan barked a laugh, "Oh my new friend, you chose to travel with us, he's your problem too now!" He gave Harmonium a winning smile, whose mouth turned up at the corners briefly as he grunted. "Actually, it will be nice not to have all the focus on me for a change. The best advice I can give you is wear the armour at night, even when you sleep. Oh, and watch out for fireballs."

At this, Harmonium laughed, and Wolfbane's face fell into a stunned expression that said: *What have I gotten myself into?*

Chapter 12
☼ A Sphinx that Thinks ☼

They travelled for two more days at a walking pace comfortable for the horses in the heat. They rested at night, shivering in their bedrolls as the temperature dropped. During the long starry nights, Lazelan had no trouble imagining himself atop Mount Embalk, surrounded by snow. The chill in the air was kept off his skin by his layer of blankets, but the cold seemed to settle right into his bones, making his teeth chatter and sending shivers up the back of his neck. The extremes of the hot days and cold nights were taking a toll on all of them. The horses, who had once stepped lively, now seemed to plod on, perhaps wishing for an end to all this sand.

On the third day, like the others, the sun baked them from overhead. Lazelan was bothered by the way the material of his clothing stuck to his body as it hung saturated with his sweat, and he kept plucking it away from his skin. They had seen nothing but the same rising and falling sandy dunes, the same sparse and prickly cacti, and the same cloudless blue sky with hardly a change. Today, the heat rose in lazy zig-zagging wisps from the tops of the dunes, creating mirages that played tricks on the eye. Lazelan had once thought that he had seen trees shading a shimmering oasis. Its beauty had taken his breath away. The sight of the pond had made his mouth begin to water in thirst, the desire to drink almost driving him to make his horse run. But he had learned not to trust what he saw in this environment.

After another long trek, he could have sworn that he could see a great pyramid rising out of the hills of sand, but he knew better and cast the vision aside as another fantastic mirage.

Finally, he decided that perhaps his eyes were not mistaken, for the pyramid grew larger as the party approached. The details of the building began to solidify as they drew near enough to see them, and more and more, he began to believe what he was seeing. The impressive structure was made out of huge sand-coloured bricks almost the height of a man. There was no discernable entrance, and Lazelan was relieved to see that the building rose tall enough to provide a vast shadow that they would be able to rest in to hide from the harsh sun.

The trio dismounted and let their horses stand in the shade of the triangular monument, giving them a bit of a respite from the heat. Wolfbane walked over to one of the pyramid's sides, inspecting the brickwork. He ran his fingers along the groove where the separate bricks met. He tested the wall and pushed against it, first with one hand, then with two. Nothing happened.

"So how do we get in?" he asked.

Lazelan looked to Harmonium to see if he might have the solution. The young mage didn't like the sparkle in the master's knowing eyes as he stood at the end of the wall and peered at something on the next side. *A door?* Lazelan wondered, *Other people? Guards?* He watched as Harmonium switched on a dazzling smile, and disappeared around the corner. Lazelan got the gnome's attention, "Come on," he urged, giving the corner of the pyramid a wide berth.

What he saw on the other side made him stop in his tracks. Wolfbane walked into him with a clattering of armour and a tiny "Oof!"

Before them were two giant statues that faced each other, almost creating an archway. The huge figures were made of packed sand, which rose up from great pedestals made of the same brickwork as the pyramid. The wall behind them seemed solid. The statues were of two gigantic winged sphinxes. They crouched majestically, lion's tails curled around their hind paws, tummies resting on the pedestals on which they perched. Their front paws curled around the edge of the platforms, but there the resemblance to a lion ended. Lazelan felt his stomach turn with anxiety as he gazed upon their very human faces. They stood still, apparently made out of the same hard packed sand as the pyramids.

"What are they?" Wolfbane asked in awe, gaping up at the sixty foot tall statues.

"Sphinxes," Lazelan remembered from his books, "they were rumoured to have the body of a lion, and head of a human."

"They were rumoured to?" Wolfbane asked curiously, "That seems pretty evident to me."

"No one has seen one alive and has lived to tell about it for hundreds of years," Lazelan informed him.

Harmonium looked from one giant sphinx to the other. He smiled and walked toward them.

"Good day!" he called loudly. His voice echoed several times, but nobody came, and nothing moved.

"Does he realize there's nobody there?" Wolfbane whispered to Lazelan. "I mean what's he trying to do, wake the house?"

"He's talking to the sphinxes," Lazelan answered him.

"Wait, he's trying to have a conversation with the statues?" Wolfbane responded confused, "Does he realize they're made of sand? Personally, I think he'll only be rewarded with *stony* silence." He chuckled to himself, "I mean I know some people can get a bit eccentric when they get older, but that's downright crazy!" Wolfbane took a moment to truly appreciate the situation, then asked the younger mage: "Well he's not going to use magic to make them *real* is he?"

"I don't think he's going to have to, look." Lazelan answered. He watched as his master walked toward the perfectly crafted pyramid wall that stood even taller than the sphinxes. His path finally made him take the first step between the statues.

The sphinx on the left moved. Sand rained down from the neck of the great beast as its head slowly turned to Harmonium Magster in all his teeny glory. Lazelan remarked that this is how Wolfbane must feel to be standing before an ogre or a giant. He kept an eye on the sphinx's gigantic paws that thankfully still remained in place.

He found the pool of energy at his core, the familiar tingling feeling rushed up his arms and neck, making the hair there stand on end. In his head, he ran through spells that he thought might work against beings made of sand. He wanted to be ready to cast at a moment's notice.

"Halt!" said a gravelly voice that made the earth seem to rumble. "No one may proceed without passing the test."

"What happens if we fail the test?" Wolfbane asked, afraid he already knew the answer. More sand cascaded to the ground from around the sphinx's mighty paw, as a set of razor sharp claws appeared.

Chapter 13
☼ A Box Within a Box/Boxing ☼

Cal woke in the silent room's crisp cool morning air. He was weary. Master Zalice's brew hadn't worked after all then. It was a pity, today was going to be a long one. He breathed up into the room to see if it would turn into a little steamy cloud that he could see in the cold. Not quite, but the chill made him want to stay in his bed where it was warm. He knew the temperature drop would make the stone floor feel freezing to his foot's touch when he finally built up enough gumption to swing his body off his straw mattress.

Where is all this hesitation coming from? he wondered as he finally peeled back his bedclothes. *Two months ago, I would have been up and dressed before the dawn on a day like today,* he thought as he changed into the outfit he would wear as a knight's squire. Today was to be the first day in his new position. He would now have more responsibility, and begin down the road to learning what he needed to know to act like a knight. He should be more excited but he was just too tired. Come to think of it, he felt down-right grumpy. *I'll have to make sure I watch my tongue today, lest it get me into trouble,* Cal reflected glumly. As if he didn't already have enough to worry about. The only time he ever got in trouble was for "giving mother lip," as father would say. Usually that only happened when he was fatigued from illness or lack of sleep. Talking back to the wrong person here though, could get him shipped back home.

He straightened his pristine green and white tunic that bore the sigil of the leafy shoot and golden sun of House Sprig. *The only thing I need now,* he decided, *is my belt.* He took a cursory glance in the trunk that lay open at the foot of his narrow bed, but didn't see it. With a sigh, he knelt and started to rummage through his clothes and other possessions he kept there. He saw the buckle poking out from beneath a shirt. Grasping the cold metal, he pulled, unfolding several of the garments within as the belt drew free. *Great, now I'll have to refold the lot.* He reached for the first piece of clothing, and removing it, uncovered an odd little box. *Strange,* he thought, *this isn't mine.*

He took up the box and regarded the metal bands across the top and the red and green jewels that decorated the bands. *Those can't be real emeralds and rubies, can they?* He wondered in amazement as the sunlight from the nearby window refracted colourful dots of red and green all over the room. *Where did this come from? It's finer than even mother's treasures.* He moved his thumb and first finger to the tiny latch that held the box shut, and jumped as a voice cleared itself behind him. His heart leapt into his throat, and it was all he could do to choke back his cry of surprise.

Cal dropped the box back into the trunk, and covered it hastily with a garment. He turned to see Augden Zalice standing in the doorway. "What was that little trinket then?" Master Zalice asked. He looked intrigued. Intrigued was bad.

"Nothing," Cal answered a little too quickly. *Act normal!* he chastised himself. "Er, that is, I'm sorry Master Zalice, I don't have time to chat, I'm in quite a rush."

"Yes," the older man let the word hang in the air. "I came to see if my tincture helped you sleep last night. I was worried when I did not find you downstairs ready to go. I thought maybe you had slept in."

"Quite so," Cal lied. Why was he lying? He

was generally always an honest boy. There was just something about the way Master Zalice had stared at his trunk, like he was trying to see through it, that put Cal on edge. "In any case, Master Zalice, I really must go." He fastened his belt around his tunic, shut the trunk with a heavy *shunk*, as if sealing the matter, and headed for the door.

Not too long after, Cal was in the caravan heading to the palace. The prince's coronation was only a couple of days off now, and Sir Stanton Sprig had been invited among others, to attend early. He had been a squire at the same time as Ormond, the kingdom's general, and they had been the best of friends. On occasions like these, it was not unheard of for Sir Stanton to get a personal invite to join the general to participate in some informal games to celebrate. This was a wonderful opportunity for Cal, who would benefit from the extra exposure to tourney practice.

Ruben, Sir Stanton's current squire, looked over to Cal. "You're not going to fall asleep on me today, are you page boy?" Cal could feel his cheeks grow hot, and he looked down at his hands, embarrassed. Sir Stanton had carried on, either oblivious, or pretending he hadn't heard at least. Cal was glad, that would have been too much. *Not unless you bore me into a slumber,* he thought scornfully.

"No Ruben," he said calmly.

The older boy snorted with derision and moved on ahead. *This is going to be a long day,* Cal thought as he watched his tormentor go. Physically, they were opposites. While Cal was sleight and average height, Ruben was thick in the chest, and had begun a series of growth spurts that had made him as tall as a horse. Cal still had the rounded face of a child, and bright wide-set hazel eyes, but Ruben sported a square jaw and had squinty mud-brown eyes that always looked too close together. The only thing similar about them was their hair. Both had ear-length straight brown hair, so that from the back, they could almost pass for brothers. That was deceptive though, because they weren't at all that close.

Ruben could be quite the bully when the mood struck him, although, there had been other times when his frankness and honesty with Cal about the job had surprised him. It was almost like getting befriended, but then Ruben would do something nasty, like the time he had saddled Cal's horse, when teaching the page to ride. He had deliberately done up the girth too loosely, so that when Cal had tried to mount his steed, the whole saddle had fallen round to the horse's side, and had spilled Cal to the ground. "Let this be a lesson to you," Ruben had instructed, "Always re-tighten the girth before you mount, you never know when a stable boy hasn't done his job."

Although he had hurt for a week, Calen had never forgotten. Cal chalked his treatment up to the fact that Ruben came to Sir Stanton from another family, and probably feared that Cal would be favoured because of his relation to the knight. It wasn't fair, but life often wasn't.

Soon, Cal would be working closely with Ruben, who would be showing him how to dress Sir Stanton for the joust or melee practice. He would just try very hard not to give Ruben a reason to make sport of him, although sometimes it seemed as though the bigger boy didn't really need a reason at all.

Chapter 15
☼ Playing *Cat*ch-Up ☼

The horrendous sound of stone grating against stone had left each hair on the back of Lazelan's neck standing on end. He looked from the sphinx's mighty claws to his master, who had frozen in his tracks. The younger mage craned his neck up to try to look the gigantic cat in the very human face. It was completely uncanny to see the herculean lion, with intelligent eyes considering him right back.

"What is this test we must pass?" Harmonium bellowed upward, his deep voice echoing slightly off the pyramid's great wall before them.

"Naught but a riddle," the lumbering voice responded. Lazelan noted that the sphinx's voice was taking on a languid quality now. Dread filled him, causing him to break out in a cold sweat despite the desert's sweltering heat. Apparently, this was all a game to the sphinx. Its voice conveyed that it was not at all worried that they would succeed.

"Well, that should be easy enough," Wolfbane declared happily. Lazelan stared at him as though he had grown three heads.

"I mean, with all of us working together, this should be a breeze. You two seem smart enough."

Lazelan was dumbfounded at his companion's cheerfulness in the face of immediate danger. He just continued to look at his friend.

"*Cat* got your tongue?" Wolfbane jested.

"Has it escaped your notice that the penalty for us failing will be our certain deaths?" Lazelan asked incredulously, wondering not for the first time if bringing him along was worth the risk he was causing to them all.

"What, can't you just conjure up some *cat*nip and-"

"Enough!" The ground shook with the lion's mighty roar. Lazelan clapped his hands over his ears to try to block out the sound until finally, the echoing stopped. The sphinx's voice returned to its former mighty rumble. "One riddle per passing must be completed, and failure results in a man that's defeated. No magic or weapon is faster than claws, or the bone crushing weight of our mighty stone paws."

"Oh great, now the giant kitty thinks it's a poet," Wolfbane announced.

Lazelan looked up nervously to see if the sphinx had heard. The big cat regarded the miniscule man as if he were a mouse it was considering having for dinner. It licked its lips. "You're almost not worth it," the sphinx mused. Lazelan's heart, which had stopped, lurched back into a steady beat.

"Well, if I'm not worth it," Wolfbane decided, and began to walk determinedly, sword drawn, right toward the spot that Harmonium was glued to. As the sword tip passed the mage, raining sand and a thunderous roar blocked out all other sound. The ground shook as the stone feline leapt, claws bared, to pounce on the mobile morsel.

This is what Lazelan and Harmonium had trained for. Both mages flew into action as the mighty cat's paws left its platform. The older mage scooped up the gnome beside him, and cast a fireball hard against the ground at their feet. *Fwoom!* The blast blew them back through the hot desert air. Lazelan took off after them, dropping his backpack to reach them quicker. His hands began to glow as he swirled them around, weaving a spell like a net above the sand that caught his two companions as they arced back toward the earth. He let them down gently, Harmonium landing on his slightly burnt feet, still holding the gnome under his arm.

It was only a split second before the cat landed, both paws covering the same spot, its accuracy faultless. When the dust in the air cleared from the cat's heavy landing, Lazelan saw the feline lift a paw to eat his prey. All that he found was a scorch mark in the sand however. He looked up incredulously at the other sphinx, who evidently had seen the whole thing. In a purring female voice, she told the grounded sphinx, "This is going to be fun. Finally, some exercise."

Chapter 16
☼ A Challenging Challenge ☼

The road leading to the castle finally broke through the foliage of the King's Forest, and all its riders had a clear view of the majesty of the palace.

The temperature seemed to rise about ten degrees with the loss of the trees' shade, and the sounds of the palace ahead were faintly becoming audible to Cal's ears. *Not too soon, either,* Calen reflected, *if I don't dismount soon, I'll have saddle sores so bad that I won't be able to ride again for a week!*

Ahead, lay the wide expanse that surrounded the castle, giving the sentinels a view of anyone that approached. Then they would just have to cross the moat that hugged the curtain walls, and their journey would be through. Cal could see from here that the drawbridge was down, and the portcullis was up, as their caravan was expected, and right on time. The castle stood ready to welcome many important people slated to arrive over the next two days. It wasn't the first time Cal had been to the palace, but each time he went, he felt dwarfed by its sheer size.

It was magnificent, with its barbican, knights' training grounds, and spectacular gardens. It had red conical roofs on its towers, and had high windows depicting scenes of multi-coloured glass over the keep's double doors. Balconies looked out over the gardens at an intimidating height, and there was a marketplace of wood and cloth stalls in the outer courtyard of the castle where merchants and craftsmen came to sell their wares.

The market seemed to call to Cal, with its mingled smells of savoury foods wafting on the breeze, and the chorus of voices singing out about their wares. He knew that once they were situated, the market was the first place he would visit. Their horses' footfalls echoed on the wooden drawbridge, and Cal looked down deep into the moat. A fish appeared to snap up a bug struggling on the surface, and in a flash of silver, it vanished again into the depths. Cal's stomach growled hungrily. *That fish would sit in my stomach pretty well right about now, I'm famished!* he realized.

He forgot about the fish almost instantly though, as his horse drew near the castle entryway. This was the part he always secretly dreaded. A shiver shuddered through him as he looked up, right at the moment that he passed under the portcullis. The spiked wooden gate was secured, he knew, but he couldn't help that split second jab of doubt that went through his mind that second-guessed whether the gate would fall as he went under. His eyes focused on the pointed ends of wood aimed at his head, and he swallowed hard. The horse in front of him wasn't moving fast enough for him, but there was nothing he could do to speed the caravan along.

Safely on the other side of the dangerous spikes, the barbican was next, a brief tunnel with holes above, where intruders could be thwarted by hot oil or arrows. The brick here was stained black, left over remnants of a thwarted castle siege that had taken place generations ago.

Once the string of horses and men had cleared the other side, Cal let out his breath in a shaky slow stream. He felt relief wash over him. *We made it!* He realized, as he saw peasants bustling back and forth, going about their daily duties.

A pretty girl carrying a basket of ripe apples caught his eye, and as he watched her go, his horse left the line and side-stepped right into the back of Ruben's steed, which had stopped short in front of him. It took a few tripping steps to recover, and came to a halt once more. Ruben turned his head and growled "Watch where you're going!" through gritted teeth.

Cal swallowed hard and stammered an apology. *This is not good, now he'll think he has a reason to come up with new cruel ways to make my life miserable*, he worried. He hoped that the pure majesty of the castle would set Ruben in a better mood. So far though, it seemed it wasn't working.

The horses were led to the stables, and the travelling party continued on foot to the knights' barracks. The boys were then sent off in different directions. Cal was sent with the trunks of clothes and personal effects to the quarters they were assigned to; Sir Stanton would stay with the other knights of the castle, and he and Ruben would be sent to stay in the quarters with the other boys that served their knights. Ruben went with Sir Stanton to the armoury. The older squire would help the knight doff his armour, and make sure the weaponry was all accounted for and mounted in the appropriate racks. Cal would deliver all of their personal affects, and would then join Ruben in the armoury to clean the travelling dust and debris from the knight's armour.

He entered the barracks of the knights, hefting Sir Stanton's things. The knights were presumably in training, as the room was empty save for one brown-haired almost scrawny boy. He was stringing a bow that looked entirely too large for him. His back was to Cal, so he needed to get his attention.

"He-hello," Cal attempted to greet him. The other boy started and whipped his head around to see who was there.

The other boy seemed to size him up, and

replied, "I think you're in the wrong place, mate, you don't look like much of a knight to me. The pages' quarters are down the path, that way." He indicated with a flourish.

Cal tried to stand up straighter. It was tough under the weight of Sir Stanton's things. "Neither do you," he replied pointedly. "I am a squire to Sir Stanton, I'll have you know," he only half lied. He wasn't sure what being able to come on this trip made him, but this kid wouldn't know the difference. The other boy rose off the bed and stood to his full height. Cal had to look up at him. Perhaps the bow was not as overly big on the boy as he had first thought. In fact, he didn't look like much of a boy now, more of a teen, really. Perhaps he was a squire too.

"I see, and just how long have you been a squire then, three weeks?" The taller boy challenged jovially.

"Actually, today is my first day," Cal admitted, giving up and looking at the floor.

"Buck up, I'm sure you'll do fine." The look of scrutiny left the teen's face, and his manner changed. "The name's Thorn, and you are?" Thorn asked.

"I am Calen, but you can call me Cal," he offered, happy to be making a friend here.

"Alright Cal, Sir Stanton, you said? You can put his things right in there." He pointed Cal toward a door along one wall that stood ajar. Preparations had been made for Sir Stanton's coming. The bed inside was made and the desk looked clean. A candle holder stood on the desk as well. Cal looked to his new acquaintance.

"I don't suppose you'd be willing to help me with these?" He hefted the things he was holding.

"Ha ha, not a chance, my friend, I am an

archer for the soon-to-be king. Besides, you'll need lots of practice carrying anything you can get your hands on to make you strong enough to handle your knight's things. Think of lugging stuff around as building character and muscle. Have you ever handled Sir Stanton's sword before?"

"No, but tomorrow I will get to learn how to dress him for battle!" Cal said excitedly. Thorn gave him a knowing look.

"Watch out for the mail, lad, it can be a real killer."

Chapter 17
☼ A Question of Entry ☼

The giant stony cat considered the three travellers. Its tail swished slowly back and forth, and with each movement, it pushed the sand into newly formed dunes around it. Lazelan knew that if they were to proceed, they would have to face this challenge at some point. He looked over at his other companions. Harmonium stood as straight as an arrow, he looked ready to take anything on. That was his way. He always appeared as a cat, seemingly relaxed, but ready to react in a split second. Lazelan had once dropped a cup of tea while supping with the man. Not only had his teacher been able to catch the cup without so much as it grazing the ground, but it was returned to Lazelan with each drop of tea still accounted for.

Now Wolfbane on the other hand, Lazelan worried about him. He didn't seem to be taking this seriously, and although Lazelan had never really seen him do anything of consequence, he would hate to see a man die unnecessarily. The gnome had simply not known what he had been getting into at the time he had offered to join them. Yet by the same token, Lazelan was beginning to fear that the tiny man might get them all killed with his nonchalance. Wolfbane noticed him staring.

"What?" he challenged.

"I was just wondering who should go first," Lazelan replied, "or if maybe we're able to answer together and help each other a bit."

"Wait," the gnome said, "You mean you dragged me out here to the middle of the desert in about a million degree heat, and you don't even know the answers?"

"We haven't heard the riddles yet, how were we to know the answers?" Lazelan questioned calmly.

"Hey," Wolfbane cupped his hands around his mouth and called up to the male sphinx that towered above them, "How long have you guarded this pyramid?"

"For countless generations," came its rumbling purr. It sounded happy about this, apparently it was not used to losing.

Wolfbane looked back to Lazelan. "There you go, countless generations. Have you ever thought about reading a book? Never enter an encounter without fully knowing what to expect, that's my motto. You guys really better be on your game, or this is going to end in a real *cat*astrophe."

Lazelan's could feel his lips press together in a thin white line of frustration. "There are no books on the subject, Wolfbane, because no one that we know of has survived to write about it."

"Well, that doesn't make our chances seem any better," He stated obviously. "Who's going first? Maybe you should. Unless that is, you're feeling *cat*atonic."

Lazelan found himself on the edge of weeping. He had actually almost laughed at that, his nerves were so far strung. They were likely about to die, and this miniature warrior didn't seem to care. *I can't think like this, he is a grown man, I have to let the chips fall where they may. I need to concentrate if I am to solve my riddle. There is no time like the present.* Lazelan thought. He knew Harmonium would want to test himself first, he cared for Lazelan, and if he failed, there was a pretty good chance that his student would too. Lazelan knew it would cut Harmonium to the bone to have to watch that. Wolfbane, on the other hand, well, Lazelan had seen him use his cunning before. He had hoped though, that the gnome would have been more helpful in this situation.

"Give us the first riddle!" Lazelan shouted upward to the human-faced cats.

The stony feline that had previously pounced, took this opportunity to stretch languidly before slowly turning to jump back on his pedestal. Lazelan didn't want to drag his death out. He wanted to get this, whatever it would turn out to be, over with. The anticipation was killing him. *Come on, come ON, COME ON!* he thought desperately.

After what seemed like a short lifetime, the sphinx seemed ready. His rumbling voice shook the earth. "You may each call out but one answer per riddle and attempt to pass."

"How will we know if we are correct?" Harmonium asked.

"You will live." The female cat replied kindly.

"And if we are incorrect?" Lazelan asked. He suspected that he already knew the end they would meet. In response, the other sphinx licked his lips and purred. Lazelan had been right, still, he shuddered. He morbidly found himself wondering if the cat would be able to swallow him whole.

The female sphinx straightened, and purred out her riddle:

"You discard the outside,
Heat the inside,
Eat the outside,
And discard the inside."

"An ear of corn!" Wolfbane answered without skipping a beat, and strode surely across the distance between the cats unharmed. Lazelan and Harmonium stared at each other, flabbergasted.

Why, Lazelan hadn't even begun to process all of the elements of the riddle, let alone been able to start thinking of a possible answer.

"How?" He demanded of Wolfbane across the span between them.

"Wait, seriously? That was easy," he answered quite sincerely. "You shuck the ear, cook the corn, eat the kernels, and then throw away the cob." He seemed shocked for a moment as he processed the fact that Lazelan and Harmonium really hadn't known. Then, signs of worry began to creep into his face. His smile faltered. "Hey guys, you can do this," he said reassuringly.

Amazingly enough, Lazelan did not feel reassured. He and the little man were going to have to have a talk. *If I live long enough to have it, that is.* Lazelan was brought out of his thoughts at the sound his master's sure voice.

"I will go next," Harmonium declared, as Lazelan had known he would. His teacher looked to the big cats and announced that he was ready.

This time, the other sphinx offered up a challenge, the tip of his tail flicking wildly, as if he were perturbed. The cat regarded the two scholars remaining, and recited ominously in his voice that sounded like rolling thunder:

> *"Some say I'm part of a free flying fowl,*
> *Though I don't make a peep,*
> *Nor hoot like an owl,*
> *I race across the land,*
> *But I don't require air,*
> *I swim through the water,*
> *But I don't get wet there.*
> *What am I?"*

The last notes of the cat's booming voice echoed off the pyramid wall and were absorbed by the sand dunes around them that were shimmering in the heat. Lazelan felt beads of sweat trickle down the sides of his face as he watched his master trying to puzzle the clues together.

Harmonium looked studious. His hand rose, palm up, to rest in front of his muscular belly. The hairs on the back of Lazelan's neck rose, and he could feel the energy draw in the air around Harmonium. This was a sensation that Lazelan was used to from years of studying around other mages. He put two-and-two together and recognized in horror that his master was about to cast. A second before it happened, Lazelan realized how the spell might be interpreted by the sphinxes. A glowing orangey-yellow light winked into existence as a miniature ball of flame was born, and hovered above his master's hand.

The glow drew the attention of the big cats and Wolfbane all at once. The little man's hand few to his sword hilt, and he began to take his first running step back toward the mages. The sphinxes were both on their feet now, ready to pounce.

In a flash, Lazelan threw up his own hands in a commanding stopping gesture, and let fly a spell of his own. Both sphinxes and the gnome froze in place; Wolfbane in mid-stride, and the sphinxes with muscles coiled and claws grasping the front edge of their pedestals. The sphinxes looked deadly, with their back ends raised, and their eyes focused on Harmonium, ready to fly from their places to land on him.

The young mage didn't want Wolfbane to try to cross back between the cats, and he didn't want to be eaten. This small fire ball was something he was familiar with, a subconscious habit of

Harmonium's that he had seen many times when his master was pondering an enigma.

"He is alright, just concentrating, he has no quarrel with you!" he bellowed up to the giant cats, "Please, don't eat us, there is no cause for an alarm, this is not an attack. Then he called across the gap to Wolfbane, "Stay where you are." Lazelan released the energy feeding his spell, and felt it snap back into the electric ball at the centre of his mind. The cats began to lower their rears, considering if what he said was true, and Wolfbane thankfully stayed put.

"How are we to know that?" The female cat inquired.

"You've seen him in action," Lazelan replied, "he doesn't take that long to act."

The cats seemed to accept this, and settled back down onto their stony haunches. The male sphinx began to lick at a paw, as if he hadn't been ruffled in the least. The female cat looked at him sideways, and a knowing grin crossed her almost beautiful sandy face. The male caught her looking and stopped licking long enough to turn his nose up as if to say *harrumph*.

The older mage stood still, head bent down, as if he had been oblivious to the whole scene that he had just been responsible for. He tended to take things in stride. The light danced over Harmonium's palm, then winked out. It reappeared, and again winked out. This process was repeated several times before Harmonium began to toss the ball back and forth from palm to palm in a small arc in front of him.

Lazelan could hear Harmonium muttering under his breath. He was saying the lines of the riddle over and over, sometimes in order, and sometimes just repeating the same phrase. The burning ball of light flew back and forth from hand to hand, faster and faster. The light seemed to grow more intense as it flew, and his words sped up as he repeated them. Suddenly, Harmonium's voice stopped. His breath caught in his throat. The fire ball floating above his palm went out as if it had been crushed in his fist as it clenched shut in triumph. He looked up to the big cats.

"Is it a shadow? A *bird's* shadow?" he asked. Neither cat showed any signs of moving or answering. Harmonium turned to Lazelan, and put a hand on his shoulder.

"There is no fault in my answer. The surety of it is undeniable. I will await you on the other side, and you *will* join me." Lazelan could only blink back unwanted tears before they fell, and nod. Harmonium had been his master, but also a father figure in Lazelan's life. He too felt sure of Harmonium's answer, but that would mean shortly having to come up with his own. He thought of his Magdolyn, and didn't want to die. Even more than that though, in this one moment, he wanted to make his master proud.

Harmonium spun his back to Lazelan and crossed the deadly sandy expanse between the two cats. He made it safely, and thus the cats turned to begin Lazelan's turn.

Chapter 18
☼ Big Sabatons to Fill ☼

Cal looked up in awe at Ormond. The man was a legend. His knightly deeds had inspired stories, ballads and poems, and he was close enough to touch! He was the man that Cal wanted to become one day, and Ormond was embracing Sir Stanton as if they had been long lost brothers. Cal felt a sense of pride at that, that *his* knight was so close to the larger-than-life man-

"...is my newest squire, Cal." Cal was broken out of his reveries by Sir Stanton's large hand clapping him on the shoulder as he introduced the boy to his hero.

"By the shields of the army of," Cal started in awe, then paused with a comically surprised look on his face, "well, you, Sir!" He finished weakly. He didn't let his embarrassment stop him for long though, before he fairly gushed at the commander. "Sir Stanton said I'm a lot like you, starting out so young and all. That made me really happy to hear, because I really want to be a knight one day. Maybe I'll even get to come here to the castle and fight under you! But I know I have to work hard Sir, and do something outstanding to work in the castle. I was wondering, Sir, is it true? Sir Stanton said you fought in a tournament when you were still a squire, and-"

Ormond put a hand up to silence him, and looking left and right, leaned in closely so only Cal could hear. "I got in a right bit of trouble for all that. You might not want to follow in *those* footsteps," he chuckled. "Perhaps one of my knights will tell you the whole tale some time, there are stories and songs written all about it. I will leave it to you to decide for yourself about which parts are true, and which are just the fanciful imaginings of a minstrel or bard."

Before he took his leave, Ormond straightened and clasped Sir Stanton's forearm, saying, "This one will keep you on your toes!" Then, to honor the wide-eyed boy, he gave Cal the knights' salute. Cal had never been formally taught the salute, but he knew exactly what to do. He laid his open palm across his heart, and extended it toward his hero, tilting his head slightly in Ormond's direction, but holding his eyes with his own. Surprised, Ormond had looked to Sir Stanton and nodded.

After the general had smiled again at Cal and had gone, Sir Stanton congratulated the boy. "Well done, Cal. You didn't even miss a beat. Your salute was crisp, smooth, and perfectly executed. I'd say you've succeeded in at least catching his eye. He may be watching for great things to come from you now."

Cal smiled, but felt himself begin to sweat. "Really? That's great," he replied, trying his best to sound enthusiastic, while he felt as though a giant had just come by and stomped all over his high hopes of a life as a knight. This was a disaster! It was only his first day as a squire, and he was fully aware that there were things he would be incapable of doing at his current size. Why, he wasn't even sure he could lift Sir Stanton's heavy armour! He was afraid that now that Ormond was watching for greatness, he might ruin his own chances by showing the general how completely inept he might turn out to be.

Stanton saw the unease on his charge's face, and tried to calm his fears. "It takes years to build up the discipline and strength of a knight. Worry not. Ormond is not going to expect a miracle of you over night. You'll learn and become more competent just as I, or even Ormond himself did." Cal began to feel a little better. "Come now," he continued, turning Cal and leading him toward the sparring grounds. "Ruben can show you the proper way to assemble my armour. We start from the bottom up, with the sabatons."

Oh, then this is sure to go well, Cal thought dejectedly. But as with every other task he had ever been given, he decided that he was going to at least try to put his best foot forward.

*   *   *

Master Zalice sat in a cart and held in his hands a little wooden box with decorated metal bands across the top. It was the same box he had procured from Cal's trunk just after the boy had left. He hadn't stolen it, well not exactly. It happened to have been his box in the first place. He had just *retrieved* it when the boy had quitted the room. Thankfully, he had been able to interrupt the child before he had had a chance to examine the contents that lay within.

Augden thumbed the latch reverently and began to lift the lid when a rather large rut in the road caused the wagon he was riding in to lurch, and the old herbologist had to slam the lid down to avoid losing his treasures.

"Watch it, you incompetent fool!" he shouted to the driver, "If I had been eating, I could be choking to death right now!"

"At least people who are choking can't make any noise," the man muttered to himself.

"What was that?" Augden demanded.

"I said I'll do my best to be more careful," the driver said to placate him.

Augden only grunted to himself in response. He had been lucky enough to catch this ride to the castle, and knew he shouldn't push his luck, even if the farmer did seem to be deliberately hitting as many bumps in the road as was humanly possible. Still, Augden had to grudgingly admit that the man was doing him this favour.

Augden had been administering a tincture to the man's wife, when the farmer had come in to let her know the wagon was ready to go with a load of fresh vegetables to the palace. Augden had casually mentioned that he had missed the chance to give a boy his much needed sleeping draught before he had unexpectedly left for the castle himself. He said that he would have gone to catch up with the boy, but his injured leg would never carry him half as far as he would need to go. He offered to waive payment his wife's tincture if the farmer would let him travel with him to deliver his vial to the boy. The farmer had gladly let him ride along, in the back, with the turnips.

Augden adjusted the uncomfortable way he was sitting. His right leg had fallen asleep as it was wedged in between two particularly large vegetables at a strange angle. He moved so that his back was to the farmer for privacy, and felt the tell-tale prickle of pins and needles as the blood started floating freely through his limb once again.

This time, he kept the box down low and close to his lap to prepare for the next inevitable bump. He let his sleeve drape over the emeralds and rubies to hide them, and opened the lid just a crack. He peeked inside and was rewarded by the glimmer of gold. He surveyed the contents, shaking the box slightly to shift some of the top pieces, so he could see what was underneath. His eyes flicked back to the gold. He needed to get rid of that, return it if possible. If he were caught with it, he would never get himself into the position of court herbologist. He might be found guilty of theft, and there was no way he was going to the dungeon. He was seeking advancement, more money, and if his plan worked, he would finally be seen in high esteem. Why, they might even give him a place in the palace, if the queen were to somehow lose her ability to cast magic. But first, he had to get in, and his key was the boy.

Chapter 19
☼ Cat Nip ☼

For a moment, the desert was silent. Lazelan could feel droplets of hot sweat trickle down his back as the sun baked his face and neck. He tried to swallow, but his mouth had gone dry, which made it a thick, slow movement way down in his throat. He longed for a drink of water, but his pack was somewhere on the dunes behind him, forgotten in their previous skirmish. He was afraid that if he walked far enough to get it, that he might just keep on going. The safety of his cabin and the warm embrace of his new wife was that way, and they called to him. It seemed like such a logical, *good* idea.

He shook his head to clear it, and wrestled his fear under control. Bringing himself back to the present, he looked up to face the sphinxes.

"Are you ready?" The female sphinx purred.

Thinking of Aylan back in Endalwynndale, his student, his queen, his friend, he felt certainty steel through him.

"No, but you better go ahead before I lose my resolve." He replied honestly.

"Very well," the cat agreed, and gave him the final riddle:

"I have more power than the Almatraek Bright,
I am darker than a cloudy, moonless night,
I Contain more evil than the Almatraek Dim,
I am more dangerous than an evil mage's whim,
Kings require me, though I am held by the poor,
And if you consume me, you shall live no more.
What am I?"

Lazelan was dumbfounded, his mind a total blank. Slowly, as if trying to think through molasses, he tried to start putting together the clues. He too repeated the lines, but found that he could only grasp at snippets of the riddle. He started to shake his head in defeat as panic began to creep in. His flesh broke out in goose-bumps, and his adam's apple began to work in his throat as he tried to force back the bile threatening to rise in his gullet. His stomach felt sick, like the time that Zaltreous had challenged him to a meat pie contest, and he had eaten way too much. He had felt unsettled and uncomfortable then, with cold sweats and a slight fever. Right now, he felt worse. Even more unnerving was the fact that his mind was still drawing a blank.

He tried repeating the lines again in his mind. *More power than the Almatraek Bright...darker than the night, more evil...more evil...*he knew he was missing pieces, but he dared not ask the cat to repeat herself. Harmonium believed in him, so he kept trying. *More dangerous than an evil mage's whim...That's Zaltreous, if it weren't for him, we wouldn't be in this mess.* His thoughts began to wander. It was easier to feel sorry for himself. He refocused and redoubled his efforts, becoming more and more frustrated with himself. *More dangerous than an evil mage's whim...what* is *more dangerous than that? What do kings require? What does the poor hold? They hold no land, that's for sure. What will kill you if you eat it? Why would a king require something like that?* He began to get confused, with all the clues starting to mix themselves up. He knew he was making mistakes. He helplessly looked up at his companions, perhaps for the last time.

Across the gap between them, Lazelan could see Wolfbane jumping up and down frantically. He opened his mouth to say something. With one swift movement, Harmonium took a knee and reached his arm around the gnome's head, securing his hand over the small man's mouth. He nodded his encouragement to his former pupil.

Lazelan squared his shoulders and asked the cats if they could repeat the riddle. The purring female voice recited it again, word for word, exactly the same as before. Lazelan tried to empty his mind of all else.

He could hear the cat's voice over and over as he thought out the riddle in an almost trance-like state. He sat on the hot sand and crossed his legs. His breathing evened out and deepened, almost like the whispers of breath coming from someone in a deep sleep. His eyelids came together, blocking out any visual input that might distract him. He sat like that for a long time. This was a trick his master had taught him. In this state, he had a heightened sense of awareness. He could find any life forces around him, or could hone his hearing to listen to a solitary grain of sand cascading down the side of a dune somewhere. This was where he needed to be.

For almost an hour, he remained motionless. Then quietly, almost as if to himself, he admitted defeat. He stood to face the cats, joints creaking from staying too long in the same position. He felt old; old, and tired. He silently said goodbye to his fair Magdolyn, and prayed that the brightness would stay with him on his journey into the next realm, whatever that would hold.

"I can't do it," he admitted.

"What was that?" the male cat straightened. He sounded excited. Across the sand, through what looked like such a short distance, Harmonium was looking at him with a hard expression on his face. Wolfbane was shaking his head no. Lazelan spoke up.

"I'm sorry, I can think of nothing," Lazelan confessed. As the words left his mouth, Wolfbane fairly went crazy, and all of the pieces clicked into place for Lazelan, like the stone spheres on a Nine Men's Morris board moving on their tracks.

The cats bared their claws, and the male sphinx licked his lips. The female almost seemed sorry, but Lazelan was oblivious.

His mind was consumed. Each line of the riddle began to make sense, the evasive word sliding into place with each phrase.

What has more power than the Almatraek Bright? Nothing. What is darker than a cloudy, moonless night? Again, nothing. What contains more evil than the Almatraek Dim? Nothing else in this world. Nothing is more dangerous than an evil mage's whim. Kings require nothing, and the poor hold nothing, that's what makes them poor. And lastly, if you consume nothing, you'll die of starvation.

"The answer is *nothing*!" Lazelan's voice thundered almost as loudly as the big cat's had. The word echoed off the side of the pyramid, and washed over them all. The sphinxes, who had bared their claws and had already begun to leap, tried to pull up short, but were already airborne.

Harmonium dropped the gnome, and began to draw energy from the sphinxes themselves to knock them out as they landed on his friend.

The sphinxes came to a stop on an invisible shield. Inside, Lazelan struggled against the weight of the giant stone felines, but he held his ground.

"Now that's more like it!" Harmonium gave his approval of his pupil's much improved shield. "If you had done that in the garden, you'd have stayed on your feet," he pointed out helpfully.

Lazelan groaned. His feet were digging into the sand, and were beginning to slip backward as he fought to hold the giant stone cats up.

"Would you mind getting them off of me?" He asked Harmonium through gritted teeth.

The groggy sphinxes were moved back up onto their pedestals where they could sleep off the rest of Harmonium's spell. Lazelan crossed to join his friends.

"Wait, you mean you could have done that at any time?" Wolfbane demanded angrily. "You made us sit here and wait, and think you were going to die, and you could have just stopped them and knocked them out?"

"Yes, of course," Harmonium answered, as if it should have been apparent the whole time.

"Then why didn't you?" Wolfbane demanded. "Why put us through all that?"

"Because that is not the way the game was played. It would not have been honorable." Harmonium schooled him.

"Besides," Lazelan added, "It might have been a *cat*alyst that could have affected the rest of our quest."

"That was a terrible joke." Wolfbane informed him.

Lazelan looked up at the peacefully slumbering felines. "Perhaps we should wake them," Lazelan ventured. They are here to protect a kingdom, it would not be fair to keep them from doing their jobs.

Harmonium copied the movements from his garden to summon any water vapour he could get from the air. He shot two blue orbs of power into the sky, right above each of the slumbering sphinxes.

"Oatasa!" *Rain!* He bellowed. The water fell, and woke the cats that were none too happy for getting wet.   The drowsiness fell away from the felines, and the male roared fit to silence an army.

Lazelan cocked a thumb at Wolfbane, and said smugly, "He did it."

Chapter 20
✪ Assembling the Knights ✪

After having some time to settle in, and being sent to the market to get some meat skewers for their lunch, Cal rejoined Sir Stanton, who was preparing to don his armour. The muscled man stood in his room within the barracks wearing a white linen shirt, braies and grey woolen chauses on his legs, and leather turnshoes. Ruben was already there, waiting with all the components of their lord's armour. They finished their light meal in minutes, Ruben glaring over his skewer at Cal the whole time.

"What are you still doing here?" Ruben whispered at Cal when the remnants had been disposed of.

"I'm to learn how to put together Sir Stanton's full harness." Cal informed him meekly.

The older boy knew better than to protest in front of his knight. There was no room for complainers in Sir Stanton's service. You had to find your own way, and take whatever was given to you. This is how they toughened you up for becoming a knight.

"Ormond has challenged me to a game of tilting at the rings today boys, so let's be quick," Stanton urged them. "You are in for a treat today; I used to be a master at this sport. Why, I might even put your hero to shame," he gloated, winking at Cal.

Cal smiled, he was excited to be able to stay and watch the match. He would have duties too, but for now they required that he stay by his knight. This day just kept getting better and better.

"Alright cur, let's see if you're the dolt I take you for," Ruben began with a sharp insult, followed by a challenge that reminded Cal just how unskilled he really was. "Which pieces go on first?"

This was going to go about as well as Cal had first anticipated. He surveyed the more than twenty pieces of armour arranged around the room, and felt at a loss. He could tell by looking at them where on the body they were to go, but no one had ever told him that there was a special order to assembling them. He had never been present to watch this before, so he had to guess. He wracked his brain to remember what Sir Stanton had said...*We start from the bottom up, with the sabatons*.

"The sabatons!" Cal cried, reaching for the shoe coverings made of connected plates of metal. They were heavy enough, but easily manageable for Cal to lift in each hand. He knelt in front of Sir Stanton and day dreamed about the flat of his lord's sword touching his shoulders in a knighting ceremony. His musings were short lived, as the sabatons were easy to fasten near the heel, and were quickly tied to points on the toes of Sir Stanton's turnshoes. Sir Stanton seemed impressed.

"Lucky guess," Ruben spat, furious that the boy had chosen correctly.

But Cal began to surprise even himself. He pointed to the next pieces that should logically cover his knight's legs. "Next should come the greaves that fit over the shins, and the cuisses for the thighs."

Cal watched Ruben wrap the greaves around the knight's shins and calves and saw how they fastened at the side where the two halves met. *Easy enough*, he thought. He went to retrieve the cuisses, and found that he needed two hands to handle each piece at a time. These were larger, and more cumbersome, with a long piece to shield the front of the thigh, and more moving plates that would cover the knee and meet the greaves. He saw that there were buckles to fasten the piece at the back of the leg. He made a move towards the knight with one of the cuisses in his hands, but was interrupted by another of Ruben's very helpful outbursts.

"You're missing something, cur. The cuisses aren't going to support themselves."

To Cal, it looked like that was exactly what they would do. His eyes passed over the remaining pieces of the suit sprawled around the room. He got distracted by the three belts lying on the bed. *Who needs three belts?* he had time to wonder before Ruben impatiently lifted the thickest of them from the bed, and buckled it around Stanton's waist. Now Cal could see more points to tie the tops of the cuisses to, which would transfer the weight of the metal pieces to the knight's hips. Without saying a word, he attached the first and then the second, so that both were suspended from the belt, and were buckled securely.

By the time he was through, Ruben had retrieved the thick shirt-like gambeson. It had almost twenty buttons to be done up the front. Ruben had already helped Stanton into the garment, and had set to work doing it up. *Man, he's fast,* Cal noted as Ruben's practiced fingers fastened button after button in the long row. Cal had to admire the teenager. If he could say nothing else nice about the boy, he had to admit that at least the bully was good at his job. The gambeson would act as padding under the mail, absorbing blows and protecting against slashes in a battle or joust. This took a few minutes to put on, and resembled a perfectly fitted dark jacket when done up.

Now it was time for the heavy mail. This was the part that that archer, Thorn, had warned him about. Sir Stanton's hauberk was a half-sleeved garment made up of thousands of interconnected metal rings. It would slip on over his head, and would protect everything between his collar and his knees. Cal tried to pick it up, but struggled with it. It took all of his strength to slide it off of the bed, where a great deal of it pooled on the floor.

"Get the armour off of the ground, cur!" Ruben bellowed, "I didn't polish it so that it would get dirty again before Sir Stanton even gets to wear it!"

Cal pulled upward with all his might to lift the mail off the floor. His muscles strained, and he grunted under the weight that didn't seem to be budging. He could feel the muscles in his forearms pull, and knew he would be sore for the next two days. He didn't care. He fought harder to lift the mail above his shoulders. His muscles began to shake from the weight. *It weighs half as much as I do!* Cal realized, and began to understand that it was much more than he could handle.

"Ruben, help him," Sir Stanton ordered. Grudgingly, Ruben slowly came to the struggling boy's rescue. He helped take up the bottom of the mail, and helped Cal to lift it above his head so that Stanton could thread his hands into the sleeves.

"Thank you," Cal said to the other squire.

"You're not the perfect squire you think you are, cur. You'll do well to remember that you can't even lift a piece of mail without me."

"And were you as skilled as you are now on your first day as my squire?" Stanton asked Ruben. "I seem to remember a time not too long after you came to me, a certain incident that happened while grooming my horse. If I recall correctly, I found you in tears and covered in horse-"

Ruben, with a slightly panicked look on his face, took that moment to cause a distraction. He was suddenly inflicted by a sneezing fit, which sounded suspiciously fake to Cal. With the first sneeze, Ruben dropped the mail he was holding, leaving Cal with the whole burden himself. Cal's arms, already shot from supporting the weight for this long, buckled under the load and started falling to the ground. Cal's hands broke out in a sweat, his palms becoming slick, *No! I can't drop Sir Stanton's mail on the ground!* he thought frantically, remembering Ruben's berating from a few minutes before.

Cal gave it one more futile shot, wrenching his tired arms upward in one last mighty heave. With surprise, he realized that the long hauberk rose a foot. *I did it!* Cal thought excitedly before the moving weight shifted back over his head. He toppled backwards with the movement of the mail, and went down hard, with all thirty pounds of the mail landing on top of him. The wind was knocked from his lungs, and Cal found he couldn't draw breath. He began to panic. *I can't breathe, get it off!* he thought frantically, but he had no air to speak. His mouth just gaped as he struggled to pull air into his unmoving lungs. Pinned like a turtle on his back, he couldn't move. Once his arms had been given time to relax upon landing, they turned to jelly and refused to do any more work for him. He struggled feebly. Ruben began laughing.

"Ruben, I suddenly find myself quite parched," Stanton commanded subtly. Ruben left to fetch some wine, still laughing. Once Ruben was gone, Stanton leaned down and easily lifted the whole mail shirt off of his new squire with one hand. "Fear not, Cal, the strength necessary will come."

Cal gasped as the weight left his chest, and his lungs gobbled the air greedily. He composed himself, taking longer and slower breaths, and pushed himself to his feet. He was determined not to give up, no matter how hard this got and he knew this was only the beginning. He was just glad that

Ormond hadn't been here to see. Stanton lifted the mail over his head and let it fall down around him, shuffling and bending a little like a caterpillar until it was in place.

"You can get into that on your own?" Cal asked in awe.

"Some of my armour, yes, but the rest I'll need help with," he said while buckling his second belt around the middle of his hauberk. "Come help me before Ruben gets back, and we'll show him just how capable you really can be."

*   *   *

As it turned out, Ruben was about to make a grave mistake. Upon entering the keep, he spoke harshly to a servant and insulted her. He demanded that she tell him where the wine cellar was. This was a very bad move. Unbeknownst to him, the servant, Millie, was the lady in waiting to the queen herself.

To her credit, Millie plastered a smile on her face, and wasted no time in giving him very detailed directions that would take him in a round-about way to the North-East tower. After following her directions in and out of rooms for a solid fifteen long minutes, he finally found the tower in question, and started down the winding stairs. The light was much dimmer here without natural sunlight showing him the way, and the burning torches held by sconces on the walls created a light so dim that it slowed his progress even more.

He cursed the servant that had obviously sent him on a wild goose chase before leading him to the cellar where the wine was stored. As he made his way deeper underground, and the air began to cool by a few degrees, he finally began to feel like he was getting somewhere, and that his task was coming to an end. Then he reached a landing on the stairs, complete with an armed guard that wanted to know what business he had descending to the royal vault.

Chapter 21
☼ No Gnome Entrance ☼

With their backs to the two giant stony sphinxes, the three travellers regarded the seamless pyramid wall. The bricks fit so tightly together that Lazelan thought he'd be hard pressed to fit even a piece of paper in between them.

"Where's the door?" Wolfbane inquired. "Surely your books and scrolls told you something about a door."

"No," Lazelan answered, "No one that we know of has ever survived the sphinxes. At least, there seems to be no record of that."

Lazelan jumped as a sudden rumbling like a rock slide erupted behind them. *The sphinx is purring,* the mage realized.

"He seems pretty proud of himself," Wolfbane remarked.

"You might be too, if you had a perfect track record," Harmonium reasoned.

"Almost perfect," Wolfbane corrected, "Until us, that is." Then he turned to address the cat. "We got past your riddles, so how about you tell us how to get in?"

"That was never part of the deal," The female cat answered in a leisurely fashion, and she topped it off with a smile that said *Good luck finding the door, buddy.*

Wolfbane blew out his breath in a huff, and leaned back on the wall to think of a way in. The wall shifted, making him lose his balance. He took a few scrambling steps backwards to catch himself, and saw the circular groove that was being left in the sand.

"You did it!" Lazelan shouted.

The sphinx didn't seem impressed. He lifted a rear leg high into the air and began to bathe himself with his back to the adventurers, apparently tuning them out. Lazelan noted that the purring had stopped.

As crack of blackness, the passage behind the swivel door began to show as Wolfbane turned to push the spot he had been leaning on. Lazelan went to help, and the great stones spun like a revolving door on an axis. Harmonium strode over to join them, though the door had moved easily enough with just the gnome pushing.

The great stone door continued to move, and the ray of light from the desert's hot sun illuminated a thin section of the tunnel that lay behind it. The edge of the light touched something slumped against the floor and far wall. The three continued pushing, and the spooky scene unfolded as the sliver of light grew to flood the hallway. There, covered in dust and cobwebs, was a skeleton dressed in ill-fitting leather armour. In one hand it held a dagger, the other disappeared into an equally dusty backpack that lay beside it on the ground. The scene grew dimmer as the sun's light began to be blocked out while the door continued to turn to shut them in.

Lazelan regarded the unfortunate figure, his eyes swooping down the leather-clad arm to the backpack. "Wait!" he yelled in a panic as he realized his satchel was still out in the sand. But the heavy stone door was on a roll, and could not be stopped so easily. It continued its slow turn. Lazelan's quick draw of energy pulled a few grains of sand from the floor as he shot out a stream to collect his backpack. The invisible force passed the two sphinxes undetected, and finding its target, began to pull Lazelan's satchel through the air at a pace almost too fast to see. The female sphinx tracked it and jumped to pounce at it like a pet attacking a string dragged before it. Lazelan saw the big cat leap in his direction, the giant face and bared claws rapidly growing closer and closer. His satchel snaked in through the crack and landed safely in his hands. The floor shook. A spray of flecks of sand hit the party as the cat landed by the turning stone door and the last sliver of light from outside was severed.

Lazelan herd something small rummaging around in the darkness. A moment later, there followed a *clack* of flint and steel, and sparks of white pierced the total darkness.

Lazelan attempted to brush off the few grains of sand that had hit him. "Let me know if you need help with that. You might want to save your supplies, in case we get separated in here."

"Separated?" Wolfbane asked.

"Fuexi," *Light*, Lazelan said in the darkness, and a ball of bright light floated over his palm. He threw it upward, and it hovered near the ceiling, its light filling the room and illuminating their path down the hallway for about sixty feet.

"How could we ever get separated in here?" Wolfbane continued, shielding his eyes from the new light source that had just destroyed his night vision. He surveyed the long single corridor. It seemed as there was nowhere else to go.

"Booby-traps," answered Harmonium sagely. He knelt to examine the dusty skeleton. Lazelan watched as the old mage of countless years gingerly lifted the flap on the backpack. Inside, the skeleton's hand grasped a disk shaped rock covered in markings. Harmonium gently lifted the the stone from between the gripping finger bones of the long dead voyager.

"What is it?" demanded Wolfbane

inquisitively.

Harmonium held it up for Lazelan to see. There were rings of markings on the stone. Each ring depicted an alphabet of some of the races of man. Lazelan recognized the Common language, Elven, Dwarven, Almatrae, and one more that he did not recognize.

"A rosetta stone," Lazelan breathed reverently. "I've never seen a real one before. It's used to decipher unknown scripts. But what is that language in the third ring?"

"Gnomish," Wolfbane and Harmonium answered in chorus.

Harmonium handed the rosetta stone to Wolfbane. "Here, stow this in your pack. Just in case we are separated, you understand."

"But if we're separated, won't you need it?" He asked before taking the offered rock.

"Harmonium speaks all of those languages, so he would have no need of it," Lazelan explained.

"Of course," he responded with an eye roll.

It was as the gnome was re-shouldering his pack that two tiny glints of green appeared down the corridor, out of the range of light. Lazelan elbowed Harmonium to get his attention.

"I know, I see them," he affirmed.

The orbs seemed to be moving toward them. Lazelan felt his skin crawl, those orbs were very uncanny. They moved slowly forward, close to the ground, dipping and floating as they approached. They began to change. Bits of black at the centre of the orbs were squeezed down to slits as the green swelled the nearer they drew to the floating light source. Then, as suddenly as they had appeared, the green orbs disappeared completely.

"Come along," Lazelan instructed, "I want to try to find something more permanent to light our way. I don't want to drain my energy with this orb, especially if I have to cast something to protect us from whatever those things were."

Harmonium quickly removed a few more items from the skeleton's bag. A rope, a short and slender carved stick, and a book all went into his own pack.

He rose, and they continued on down the corridor toward the place where the orbs had vanished.

Chapter 22
☼ From Past to Present ☼

Cal was just picking up Sir Stanton's helmet when Ruben finally returned to the room, still empty handed. The armour that had still been laying on the bed when Ruben left, was now being worn by the knight. The cuirass, arm harnesses, green and white surcoat, sword belt, and gauntlets, were things that a knight had to have help donning due to the places and way they were pointed or buckled. The fact that they were on properly was a testament to Ruben that Cal had done his job well.

"Ah, Ruben, just in time," Stanton welcomed him back. "Prepare my horse and meet me at the training arena."

The teen began to explain, "Yes, Sir, I come without wine though, I-"

"No matter, my horse please, Ruben. I'm sure Cal will be up to the task of getting me something to quench my thirst. I will need it once the tilting begins." Stanton nodded to dismiss them both. The older boy dealt Cal a painful punch to the shoulder on the way out of the barracks.

"Stay out of my way, cur!" Ruben barked angrily.

Cal rubbed his sore shoulder as he made his way to the keep. *Ouch! What did I ever do to you?* he thought miserably at the older boy's back. He felt very alone. He hadn't done anything on purpose to offend Ruben, he had only done his best at his job. That was the reason he was here, and he wasn't about to stop that. How was he supposed to stay out of the older boy's way when they were going to have to spend the next few years working with one another? When Ruben had left Cal holding the much too heavy hauberk, he had honestly worried that he might die. In the midst of fighting for his breath, Calen had felt like he was drowning with the water pressing down on him. Now, he only hoped that Ruben wouldn't decide to pull a more dangerous stunt that might actually harm him, or worse.

*   *   *

The cart carrying the farmer and Augden Zalice merged with a long caravan of wagons heading to the castle. There was a line that backed up well into the king's forest, as people presented themselves and their wares to be allowed through the palace gates. *I'll make better headway on foot, even with my bum leg.* Augden decided. He hopped off the back of the wagon with the turnips and bid the farmer adieu.

He hobbled along the side of the row of wagons and carts until he came to a more hospitable and noble looking carriage. He followed it closely, trying to glean from the conversation of its inhabitants who might be inside. Perhaps they would be his next target.

Snippets of conversation wafted out in hushed tones. It sounded like a plan was afoot.

"We should take the opportunity now!" A male voice argued emphatically.

"Flanx," a woman's voice purred in a tut-tut tone of voice. "I know the coronation seems very convenient, but we need to wait until Zaltreous is with us. He will be an extra pair of eyes, if nothing else. Consider the fact that they will be surrounded by their officers who will be on the alert for a possible attack, and with so many witnesses, you never know when someone might try to interfere. Not to mention the fact that the queen will be there too," the female voice reasoned.

Flanx? Augden's attention had been hauled into focus when he had heard the name. *How many men named Flanx can there be?* He realized that he knew the owner of the male voice he was hearing.

"Ah yes, the mage, don't worry, I can take care of her," Flanx replied confidently.

Yes, come to think of it, I even recognize his voice! Augden thought with relish. *Oh, this will be good.* It was always a positive thing to have a secret, or a bit of leverage on a person tucked away in case you ever had need of it.

"We will stick to the agreed upon plan," the woman said sharply, "If you want to go all rogue on me, Flanx, then I'll turn around now and go back. You won't get past the gatehouse without my invitation," she threatened.

"As you wish, Milady," Flanx replied. His voice had a strained tone to it, like it was being forced between gritted teeth.

There was a brief shuffling sound, and the carriage swayed slightly as a bent over man in a long white robe stepped down onto the ground in front of Augden.

"Why that wouldn't happen to be Flanx, now would it?" Augden hailed him with a warm and welcoming voice.

Flanx's head quickly turned to find Augden, and his face relaxed immediately. "Oh, It's you," he replied, almost dismissively. He began walking behind the wagon, trailing it like a servant should. "I'm sure that I recognize you from somewhere..." he let his voice trail off. He seemed somewhat preoccupied.

"You used to come to get herbs from me, before you were shipped off, I mean decided to travel." Augden replied almost smugly.

"Yes, now I remember," the old man said

dryly. "How did you get an invitation to the coronation?"

Now it was Augden's turn to feel flustered, but he tried to answer as smoothly as he could. "I didn't, but I have a tincture for one of the squires inside. He left without it, and I'm sad to say he won't be able to function without it."

"And he still might not," Flanx mocked, "Unless the boy has realized and has told the gatehouse guards that he is expecting you. No one may enter unless they are on the list. The castle has really cracked down on security for the big event. No one unexpected gets in or out."

"Well then, clearly, I am with you." Augden replied matter-of-factly.

The thin man with the long white hair and robe started laughing what sounded like a real hearty belly laugh. "I think not." was his dry response at the end of it all.

"I see. Alright then, I suppose I will be forced to continue on ahead to see if there is another kind soul that will add me to their entourage. When I get to the gate, I'll be sure to tell the guards just how safe the king and queen will be in your hands." Augden informed him with a conspiratorial wink.

"I can assure you, that the king and queen will be perfectly safe." Flanx responded.

Does he look a little nervous? Augden thought to himself with quite a bit of satisfaction. "Yes, I heard." he confessed happily.

"That is to say, Lady Aurastia and I would be simply delighted to have you accompany us," Flanx invited grudgingly. "Now you just stay close to me, until we are through the gate."

Augden trusted the other man about as much as a tree trusts a hungry beaver, in other words, not at all. Having said that, this was Augden's way past the guards. Once inside, there was no telling what would happen. If Flanx and his mistress were up to no good and the queen was somehow harmed, well then, perhaps the way would be clear for Augden's advancement. Augden didn't know who this lady was but that was neither here nor there. All that mattered was that she was a noble.

He decided that he was going to have Cal steal her signet ring, as he had the others. Normally, he would not target someone that could identify him, but Flanx had always been snobbish, and besides, it was always good to have an insurance policy in case the other man decided to cause problems for him once they were inside.

Chapter 23
☼ Turnabout is Fair Play ☼

As Lazelan, Harmonium, and Wolfbane followed the glowing orb deeper into the shadowy corridor, Lazelan realized that there was a ray of light ahead. When they got close enough, Lazelan let his orb go out. He looked up to investigate exactly what it was. It seemed to be a perfectly square little shaft in the ceiling that afforded just enough light to see in a five foot radius where it hit the floor. "

"Hey guys, look at this," Wolfbane urged.

Lazelan saw his small companion facing one wall, where markings were carved into the stone in rows. He recognized it immediately.

"I'm guessing that whatever this is, you can read it," Wolfbane hedged, looking to Harmonium.

"Yes," he replied, this must have been why the adventurer had had the stone. He was no mage.

"How can you tell?" Wolfbane inquired.

"That message is written in Almatrae, the language of magic. Any mage would be able to read that, only someone without any magical ability would need something to help him translate it." Lazelan explained.

"Curious," pondered Harmonium out loud.

"What?" Wolfbane demanded.

"We shall see," the old mage responded cryptically.

"Wait, you can't leave it like that!" Wolfbane insisted, "What will we see?"

"The master rarely speaks on a subject unless he is completely sure of something," Lazelan told him.

A loud and sudden hiss came from the dimness of the corridor, interrupting them.

"Lazelan, what does the message on the wall say?" Wolfbane asked quickly. Lazelan thought he heard a slightly frightened edge to his voice. Wolfbane drew his dagger and spun to see where the next hiss was originating from. Perhaps Lazelan wasn't imagining it after all.

"It's another riddle," Lazelan mused, admiring the perfectly straight script that must have taken hours or days to chisel into the wall. *What would have happened if the person made even a simple mistake?* However long this had taken, the result was flawless.

He read the lines on the wall aloud for the gnome, who had gotten quite jumpy.

> "*Ey jaxa ira so rat,*
> *Umekut so dir ot hix so ina*
> *Ey jaxa arta tay tara sinatayt kalifae,*
> *Ser sul arau relik tanekae.*
> *Ey tajaraux jaro ha iyatfuesayt oaxir,*
> *Bod taja jarotari ha sitae lot fue.*"

No sooner had he finished, then a third hiss sounded, closer this time. It brought with it the reappearance of those two glowing green orbs a long way down the hall, but now visible. They hovered an inch apart, and a foot off the floor again, and moved quickly down the corridor toward them.

"What does that mean?" Wolfbane begged almost desperately.

"Wait, you were fine with the giant sphinx, but whatever that is scares you?" Lazelan asked skeptically?

"I can't help it, little creepy things set my nerves alight!" Wolfbane insisted. "Now, the writing on the wall, what is it? Hurry!" The orbs were about fifty yards away, and glowed intensely.

Lazelan translated:

"I can turn the world around,
Without the need to touch the ground.
I can show you both our faces,
Or just empty open spaces.
I won't think on yesterday's plight,
But will reflect on things so bright."

"A mirror!" Wolfbane cried. The glowing orbs sped up, now only twenty-five yards from them. They now appeared as two horizontal ovals bisected by a black line, and they kept coming. "Ah! Why didn't it work? We should have gained access to another hidden door, or those *things* should have stopped, or something!" he gibbered. "Wait, what's mirror in that language of yours?" he fairly squealed as the orbs got closer and closer. Another hiss echoed off the confining walls, very loudly now. "Quickly, man!" Wolfbane ordered.

Wow, he's really losing it! Lazelan reckoned. *I wonder if I should tell him that it's only an illusion.*

"Thinking for you really is like wading through mud, isn't it?" Wolfbane jibed in desperation. "And you're supposed to be his star student?" He asked, cocking a thumb toward the older mage, who was also just standing around, too calmly for words.

On second thought, Lazelan decided, *maybe I'll just let him sweat a little.* "Mud?" Lazelan asked, cocking his head and crossing his arms in front of his chest. The greenish ovals were gaining momentum. First twenty yards away, then fifteen.

When no further answer came from the red-headed mage, the disturbed little man supplicated to Harmonium. "Please, help him out. What's the word? *Please?*"

"I think you should apologize to my friend," Harmonium insisted. The bright floating ovals were only ten yards away now, and Wolfbane had started to shift his dagger from one hand to the other out of nervousness. He had crouched slightly in the direction of the ovals, as if ready to meet them.

"I'm sorry, I'm *sorry!*" he bellowed. "Now for the love of all that is bright, please tell me the word!"

"Rotari," Lazelan finally acquiesced.

A great crunching sound paired with a squealing of metal on metal filled the corridor as a big disk mounted on the wall began to turn. The back side was polished, and turned to face the shaft of light coming in from the ceiling. It reflected the beam down the hallway toward the approaching ovals, and as light washed over them, Lazelan saw the appearance of the head of a black cat. The orbs had been its green glowing eyes in the darkness, and its sleek body now shone as it continued to approach. It hissed again, the fur on its back standing on end, and in the last few feet of its approach, it leapt straight as Wolfbane's face.

The very manly armoured gnome screamed like a little girl and slashed out wildly with his dagger, while the cat passed right through him and continued on down the hallway in the direction they had come, hissing all along the way.

The two mages broke out laughing, leaning on each other for support. Wolfbane straightened, confused and more than a little embarrassed. "What was that thing, a ghost?"

"An illusion," Lazelan informed him. "It must be their version of a warning to scare off intruders that might wander in while the sphinxes are napping or are off hunting. I'd say for most, it would have worked."

Wolfbane straightened, and re-sheathed his dagger. "I knew that," he stated unconvincingly.

"Uh-huh," Lazelan chortled, "sure."

"Let us never speak of this again," Wolfbane requested hopefully.

"Of course not," Lazelan tried to say with a straight face. He was fighting off the next bout of laughter, trying to choke it back for Wolfbane's sake. Lazelan almost felt bad for him...almost. He decided he would honor his friend's request, but couldn't resist one last opportunity to rub it in. "That would be very *catty* of me."

"Everyone's a jester," Wolfbane muttered as the group bravely began to follow the beam of light down the hallway toward the unknown.

Chapter 24
✧ Sleep Walk ✧

The moment Augden Zalice had made it past the castle guards, he had gladly left the company of Flanx and his mistress. He hadn't known what brand of no good the old man had been up to and he hadn't much cared, as long as the elderly man hadn't tried to tangle Augden up in it too. He had had bigger fish to fry. Augden had gleaned which inn they were housing in, and had taken off in search of Cal.

Augden had finally tracked the boy down at the tilting of the rings, and had made plans to see the boy before he rested for the night. Then, he had made his way to inn after inn, looking for a place to stay. It had put him in a rotten frame of mind. Every room seemed to have already been taken by people who had flocked to the castle to witness the coronation. He had already tried The Spacious Satchel, The Iridescent Iris, and The Roomy Sour Puss inns. He had even traversed the seedier sections of taverns with rooms to let. Finally, the barkeep at the Rampaging Old Bear, had told him that although his rooms to let were full, Augden would be welcome to stay in the storeroom for a price, provided he left the stores alone. Augden had gratefully accepted, and had bedded down on a blanket to wait for nightfall.

Augden woke with a start, his heart pounding in fright.

Thud, thud, thud, came the sudden sound again; a meaty fist pounding on the storeroom's wooden door. This time, a voice followed.

"Are you up in there? You said you wanted to be woken as the sun went down. That would be now." Augden recognized the barkeep's deep voice.

"I am up, with thanks," Augden shouted back. He heard footsteps retreat back to the bar. As Augden moved, he felt as though his joints were creaking. His leg was still stiff and sore, not healing at all fast enough for his liking. He pulled his leather bag over to where he sat, and rummaged around in it for a poultice that he had made for his injury. He dabbed a bit of the paste on his leg, and worked it into the skin over and around his knee. The flare bark in the mixture began to heat up, soothing the joint, and the mint followed with a cooling effect. *What absolute bliss.* Augden sat back for a moment, just enjoying the reprieve from the pain.

After granting himself a few moments to relish it, he pulled himself to a standing position with the help of his staff. The aching came back, but at least it wasn't as bad now.

He made his way to where Cal was preparing for sleep. He entered and saw a second bed with a motionless form under a thin blanket. He hadn't been expecting anyone else in the room. This could be bad.

"Shh," Cal warned, "Ruben is sleeping, and I'd rather not have him wake up."

That's alright then, Augden thought, relieved. He sat at the foot of Cal's bed, and pulled out the familiar purple medicine that was supposed to help the boy sleep. In reality, it was basically just a very poor wine with some spices added, but Augden needed the boy to believe it would make him sleepy; the mind was a very powerful thing, and he wanted it working for him. Cal took the vial of liquid reluctantly, and held onto it.

"Do I have to drink this, Master Zalice? I really don't think it's working very well. To tell you the truth, every time I take this, I wake up feeling more exhausted than even the longest sleepless nights." Cal begged.

Oh no, you're not doing this now when I'm so close to having everything I need! Augden began to panic inwardly, but told Cal in a regrettable voice, "Oh Cal, you should have told me, I should have made the draught stronger if it wasn't working. Give it here." Cal handed it back, a satisfied expression on his face. *Oh, you're not getting off that easily, we're not quite done yet, my boy.* Augden thought as he unstopped the lid of the vial. He removed a pouch from his bag, which contained a brown powder. He extracted a pinch of the ground up cloves, and added them to the tincture. Then, he replaced the stopper and gave the vial a good shake. He held it up, and watched the little bubbles that had formed at the top pop one by one.

"There, that should do it," Augden reassured him as he handed Cal back the potion. *The cloves will do absolutely nothing for you,* Augden knew, *but I think they're about to go a long way toward helping me!*

Cal looked at the purple liquid skeptically. "Bottoms up!" Augden encouraged, "This should make you sleep like a baby and awaken refreshed." The boy plugged his nose and downed the contents of the vial. By the time he was done, Augden had his trusty silver coin already beginning to move across the backs of his knuckles.

The boy's eyes followed the coin back and forth, back and forth. Augden watched for the telltale droop of the boy's lids, and coaxed him with his voice. "Your lids are getting heavier, it's hard for you to hold them open. Take a deep breath, feel free to let your lids close." It was only a moment longer before the boy's eyes shut completely.

Augden continued in a silky smooth voice, "You find yourself at the top of a staircase, and you will start to descend, one step at a time. With each step and each deep breath, you will sink farther into a deep sleep. Take the first step now; one, you are feeling more *relaxed*. Take another; two, you are *drifting* more *deeply*. Three, you can feel your *muscles relax*. There is no more tension or pain. Four, you feel *calm...*"

Augden continued until the boy was at the bottom of his subconscious staircase, and was in a very suggestable state. "Now, this is exactly what I want you to do," Augden began. He gave the boy his orders, and finished by assuring him that when he woke, he would feel as if he had had a good night's sleep. He hadn't bothered to do this in the past, but decided it was probably necessary. If another mistake was made, he would need the boy to think the potion had worked in order to be able to put him under once more. The boy had been very reluctant to take the potion this time as it was. If all went well tonight though, Augden wouldn't have to rely on the boy again.

*　　　*　　　*

Sometime later, an owl hooted in the darkness outside, and Calen's eyes opened once more. Master Zalice was gone, the squires' candle had been blown out, and Ruben slept on, but Calen's mind registered none of it.

He went to the trunk at the foot of the bed, and changed into the dark clothes he found there. He added the pouch to the belt at his waist, and rummaged through his things until he found the little wooden box. It silently went into the pouch, and he stole out into the night.

Chapter 25
✿ A Ringing in the Night ✿

Ruben threw back the covers and leapt out of bed to pursue the cur as soon as he had left the room. *What amount of no good is he up to now?* the teen wondered. *Whatever it is, I don't want it to reflect on me. I've worked hard for too long to have this whelp ruin House Sprig with his actions.*

He had hated Cal from the very first time he had laid eyes on him. He was the lord's nephew and as such, Ruben knew that he would be favoured, even over the other workers that had proven their worth for years. It wasn't right. Ruben didn't care if the boy took to being a page like a horse pulling a cart. A person had to earn respect in this world, it wasn't just automatically given to them, no matter who they were.

He snuck along behind the boy, sticking to the shadows to avoid notice. The cur was pretty good at sneaking, Ruben had to admit, he almost lost the boy a few times himself, and Ruben prided himself on his tracking skills. The two boys travelled through the closed down marketplace, with shutters drawn and wares tucked away, and made their way to the Spacious Satchel Tavern and Inn. *What in the world could he need here?* Ruben was mystified. *The place is all closed up; every one of the staff has long gone to sleep.*

Ruben watched as the cur circled around to the back of the inn, and peered in through the shutters of the second window that he came to. He opened the shutters, and in one smooth movement, grabbed the top of the window and swung his legs inside to land on his feet with only the most minute *thud* as his toes touched down.

How did he do that? Ruben gawked in amazement. He waited until the cur had moved away from the window, and then got closer so he could peer inside. He watched, unbelieving, as the smaller boy went to the room's tiny table and picked up what appeared to be a man's signet ring. *A thief?* Ruben speculated, *I don't believe it. A suck up maybe, but not a thief. The cur is just too kind to everyone. He needs some real hardening up to make it as a knight, but this? I wouldn't have believed he had it in him if I hadn't seen it with my own eyes.*

The bow drew a decorated wooden box from his black pouch. *By the shields of the army of Ormond, where did he get that?* The boy opened the lid and took a ring sized for a lady's finger from the box. He went to the travelling chest, and lifted the lid. S*cree!* Ruben bit his lip as the hinges squealed loudly in the dark room. The man on the bed had been snoring, and now the snoring hitched. The boy inside worked quickly now, rummaging in the trunk until he lifted a lady's gown. He dropped the ring up the long sleeve of the garment, and hastily folded it back the way it had been. *Is he planting the ring, or returning it?* The man's snoring had just begun to resume when the the cur closed the lid and it repeated the loud and eerie sound, *scree!*

The man in bed stopped snoring again and started to mumble something to his wife, asking if she had heard something. When she didn't answer, He began to sit up to better look around the room. The cur dropped instantly, and Ruben spun backward away from the window, so his back rested against the wall beside it. Cal was going to be stuck inside. If he was discovered, it would create a dark opinion of House Sprig, and Ruben simply couldn't have that.

He had to do something to get the boy out of

there, but what? He looked up to the full moon that had been lighting their way, and it came to him. He hooted quite expertly like an owl. He left a few moments of silence, and hooted once more. The deep male voice inside muttered something, and Ruben heard the welcomed sound of the bed creaking as the big form rolled over and settled in once again to sleep. Ruben was beginning to turn once again to survey the scene inside, when Cal's black-clad body came sailing out of the window head-first. The smaller boy landed on his hands and rolled into a summer-sault to absorb the flying force. He popped up neatly to his feet, and began running off again.

Ruben was in hot pursuit. This time, he planned on stopping the other squire before he could get them both caught, and the house they served in trouble. The quick boy flitted down an alley between two low buildings, and Ruben was forced to change his course at the last second to keep on the other boy's trail. As a result, he smacked his shoulder painfully off the corner of the building as he turned down the alley. *Ow!* he swore in his mind, *For every bump and bruise I get while chasing you, cur, you'll get one to match, I swear!*

Ruben caught up with the smaller squire as he was about to exit the alley and grasped his shoulder from behind to halt him.

"Now I've got you, cur! We are going back to our room before you cause any more mischief," he berated the young boy. "As a squire, you represent House Sprig. Everything you do reflects on our lord, our lady, and the rest of us!"

Cal was blinking, and was looking very confused, as if beginning to come out of a daze. He put a hand to his head.

"Are you even listening to me?" Ruben

demanded. He shook the smaller boy, hard.

"Whoa," the cur exclaimed, almost losing his balance. Ruben was confused, this was not the nimble boy he had seen a moment before. "What are we doing out here?" It seemed to Ruben as if the boy's speech was soupy and unsure.

"Come on," Ruben ordered, beginning to lead him back to where they belonged. The older squire was very confused now. The cur genuinely didn't seem to know where he was or what he had been doing, and he was moving very slowly, like someone who was fighting to awaken from a deep dream. For the first time, Ruben took pity on the boy, "Let's get you back in bed." But, he swore to himself that he would get to the bottom of this whole thing.

When they got safely back inside their room, Ruben sat the younger boy down and questioned him. "What did you think you were doing out there? Where did you get that box? Did you steal it?"

The boy looked lost and tired and confused. "I thought you brought me outside!" the boy insisted, "and what box? I've never stolen a thing in my life, I'll have you know!" he reported grouchily. "Ruben, this whole charade isn't fair, you dragging me outside in the middle of the night to tire me out so I'll mess up tomorrow. You know that I've been having trouble sleeping, I've even been taking Master Zalice's awful medicine, not that it's helping any."

Ruben felt a jolt of understanding. "Did Master Zalice visit you tonight?"

"Yes, with a sleeping draught," the boy replied. Ruben made him upend the pouch that still hung at the other boy's side, and the box with the rubies and emeralds set into the lid tumbled out onto the bed.

"I suppose you're going to tell me that you've never seen that before?" Ruben asked.

"I have seen it, but I don't know how it got here. I found that same box in my trunk in my room back at the manor," Calen told him, "In fact, I discovered it just as Master Zalice came to see if his last potion had worked. I didn't know what it was, so I hid it away until I could find out. It should still be there." All the tiredness had now gone from the younger boy's voice, and Ruben could tell that he was piecing things together. The older boy picked up the box and handed it to the younger.

"I think that we should open it," he advised.

*   *   *

Something was wrong. Augden stood at the window of his storeroom back at the Rampaging Old Bear, waiting for the boy to deliver his box. Augden's knuckles were going red, as he knocked them in an impatient rhythm against the sill. This was taking too long. Something had definitely not gone according to plan. The not-knowing and the waiting were killing him. He felt like calling Calen's name into the night. He wanted to go find the boy and demand why he was late, but that wouldn't happen. That would expose Augden, and he wouldn't risk that. It was just impatience getting the better of him, he knew.

He had seen the box in the boy's hands in his room back in Elbon, and had feared that he had been found out. However, Augden had been able to recover his box, and everything had seemed to be intact. It had been a close one, so now he was jumping at shadows. After tonight's activities, the boy was to have brought Augden's things back to him before returning to bed to sleep the rest of the night. That's exactly what Augden believed would happen.

Another half hour passed, with Augden's suspicions mounting. His imagination was coming up with worst-case scenarios that repeated over and over in his mind. *What could have possibly happened?* he wondered desperately.

Not long after, a rooster crowed a welcome to the rising sun, and still the boy hadn't come. Augden began to pace back and forth in the tiny room, and started to formulate a new plan.

Chapter 26
✪ Trapping In Depth ✪

Lazelan and Harmonium walked shoulder to shoulder, following the gnome and the beam of light down the corridor that seemed to go on forever. The excitement that Lazelan had felt when they had gained entrance to the pyramid was starting to wane. His master's lectures about the Embralish people had fascinated him in school, but as they continued to follow more and more of the same thing, he began to get bored. At first, he had had his guard up, eyes constantly shifting around, looking for signs of booby traps. He had stopped bothering to look about fifty yards past. His mood was becoming disheartened by the time he realized that they were heading to what appeared to be a dead end.

When they got closer, however, Lazelan realized that it was a corner, with another one of the polished metal disks refracting the light down a new hall. There didn't appear to be any doors, just another continuous corridor.

"Are you still afraid that I'm going to get lost?" Wolfbane asked dryly. "I mean, this corner, it looks a bit tricky. I can't tell you how long it's been since I've turned left."

"You might want to wait before you try that tricky corner, look." Lazelan pointed out, staring at more carvings on the wall. These ones appeared to the left of the opening for the new hallway. "I think we're meant to figure this out before we enter."

Wolfbane rubbed his hands together excitedly, "Alright! I haven't had this much fun in ages. Lay it on me."

Harmonium read the Almatrae script carved by the entrance to the new hall:

"*Tarae nivear Ey ru,*
bod Ey tast rau kusruf,
Tarae sara Ey umek gurdae
kul kae postik takiyat taritae jarot,
Ey postik tari bala,
Dod rau bal ser tab,
Est tati Tay tas sauxgartaiyat,
Ey taja fal umek tari su."

Lazelan automatically translated it for Wolfbane, and expected an immediate answer:

"*Some call me spring,*
But I am no season,
Some pair me with bridges
When they've lost all reason,
I have a landing,
Yet no stair or wall,
And if you're unbalanced,
I'll end with a fall."

His last words echoed off the wall, and then there was silence. Lazelan looked down at Wolfbane, surprised that he hadn't blurted the answer right out like he had with the others. Wolfbane remained silent. He seemed to be inspecting the floor with great interest.

Great, not only has he decided not to help, he's ignoring me too. Alight, I guess we're on our own. Lazelan knew that meant that he was going to have to figure it out by himself. Harmonium was a good teacher, and as such, was never one to just give the answer away. Lazelan was going to have to do some serious thinking. His mind cringed. He was very adept at magic, and herbology, but language games were very tricky for him. He just wasn't good at them.

He read the chiseled wall to himself again. Then he read it out loud a second time, and a third, and a fourth. *This is hopeless, I just don't get it!* He looked down at Wolfbane again, hoping with all his might that the the little man would give him a hint or some kind of clue. The gnome looked up at him and smiled.

"I'm tired of doing all the work, I thought I'd let you have a go," the gnome insisted. Anger flashed up inside Lazelan.

"Doing all the work? So I guess all the spells I've been using to light the way, and keep you *alive* don't count for anything?" Lazelan asked incredulously, taking a step toward the gnome. He hadn't realized that his hands had balled up into fists until Harmonium put a hand on his shoulder to stay him.

Lazelan looked to who was restraining him, and snapped out of it. He let his hands relax, and he apologized to his short friend.

"That was a dangerous game you just played," Harmonium scolded the gnome, then he moved his attention to his former student. "But, he was right." Lazelan gaped at his teacher, and helplessly began to look back toward the writing on the wall. Harmonium drew his attention back before he got a chance to start reading again. "Look at me." Lazelan looked his master in the eye. "Now, keep your eyes on me. Remember the candle? I am your candle right now. Now what is the answer to the riddle?"

Lazelan remembered a trick Harmonium had taught them in class, to focus their minds enough to cast silently. Saying an invocation was much easier than simply thinking it. You had to lend the thought power. It took way more concentration, because you had to focus on what you were casting the spell on, as well as imagining the words. They were given homework to try to put out a candle using magic, without saying a word. The candle acted as a focus point, and in the dark room, it drew your attention easily for there was nothing else that you could see to pull it away.

Lazelan looked at his master and thought through the puzzle. *Some call me spring, but I am no season.* **What's another word for spring? A coil is a spring. Spring can also mean to jump.** *Some pair me with bridges when they've lost all reason.* **I haven't heard of a coil on a bridge. But people can jump off a bridge, in fact, when people get angry or frustrated, they often tell people to do just that. That must be it! What's the last part?** *I have a landing, yet no stair or wall, and if you're unbalanced, I'll end with a fall.* **When you jump, you land, hence the landing, but if you lose your balance or stumble when jumping, you can easily fall. That's it, it all fits!**

"I believe the riddle refers to jumping," he guessed. He explained his reasoning to his peers. Normally, he would look to Harmonium for confirmation, but this time he looked to Wolfbane to see if he was right. The gnome was beaming.

"I knew you could do it," he congratulated the mage. "Now, what do you think it means?"

"Perhaps it is a riddle to guide us," Harmonium suggested.

"Or hinder us," Wolfbane countered.

"The riddles so far have helped us at every step of the way," Lazelan pointed out. They allowed us to pass by the mighty sphinxes, and solving the last one afforded us the light we desired. Perhaps this is a clue to safe passage down the hall."

The three stood in silence regarding the doorway and hall beyond it.

Lazelan needed to find out whether the wall had been a trap or not. He thought for a moment, and unshouldered his satchel. He considered it as he hefted it in his hands, and then he pitched it down the hall. It cleared the first couple of stone bricks in a slow arc, and landed unceremoniously, rolling through the wisps of sand down the hall. It came to a stop. Nothing else happened.

"So…" Wolfbane let his voice trail off.

"The hallway looks pretty safe," Lazelan concluded. "Let's go."

"You first," the gnome offered very politely.

"Well, technically, the bag already went first," Lazelan pointed out, "The next person would be second. There were no deadly flying darts or puffs of poison gas, we should be fine!"

Wolfbane stood as tall as he could, crossed his arms over his chest in a this-conversation-is-over stance, and said "Then you had better *jump* to it."

Behind him, Harmonium chuckled. Lazelan

turned to offer to let the old man go first, but he could tell by the look on his master's face that he shouldn't even bother.

Lazelan was no coward; he'd gone up against an angry five headed dragon, another powerful arch mage, and hadn't batted an eye when he had to jump in against the sphinxes. The difference here was books, or rather, knowledge. He had read about the others and learned about them at the university. Here though, he felt totally out of his depth. He was fairly apt at reading body language, mages learned to become good at this very quickly. Sometimes the body would give away a thought before a word was said, and this skill was tremendously helpful in a mage to mage duel. He couldn't read a hallway though. There was no information an any textbook about the correct way to navigate this pyramid, or what types of traps awaited those who tried. He really just felt helpless. *I have to succeed, Oslan needs me to find that book,* he thought.

Lazelan backed up a pace and took a deep breath to steel his nerves. He was literally jumping into the unknown. He tried to aim for the spot where his satchel had landed, and leapt across the first four foot block that made up the floor. *I'm not going to make it!* his mind roared with the realization that his feet were going to come down square in the middle of the second block. He screwed his eyes shut. *May brightness be with me,* he had time to pray as first one foot, and then the other landed. His eyes flew open and he was forced to take a couple of running steps, but nothing seemed amiss. *I did it!* Lazelan elated as Wolfbane cheered at the doorway.

Without missing a beat, Harmonium gracefully soared over the questionable block and landed expertly, keeping his balance even when his feet skidded on the other side. The older mage stopped and looked back at the gnome, who had backed all the way cup to the wall behind him. He took a running start and jumped when he reached the doorway.

He almost made it. His two small feet landed hard at the same time, right across the seam where the first and second sand coloured blocks met. There was an audible echoing *clack*, and first set of blocks began to move. They fell away from under the gnome's heels, and he was left teetering over the black space behind him. He started to fall backwards, arms pin-wheeling wildly as he tried to shift his center of gravity forward.

Harmonium leaned forward and grabbed the upper edge of Wolfbane's leather armour. For a moment, the gnome stayed there in limbo, half on, and half falling off the stone edge. Now his arms stopped, and grabbed at Harmonium like a drowning man clutching for the only thing that could keep him afloat. The mage yanked him forward, hard. His armour, pack, and body all shifted, and the gnome's feet met with solid ground.

From behind him came the sharp *TROCK, Trock, Trock, trock*, of stone hitting brick, a sound that was growing more distant by the second.

"The rosetta stone!" Wolfbane lamented. "It was at the top of my pack. What will we do now?"

Lazelan answered as he carefully edged over to the hole in the floor. He peered into the abyss, and he felt unsettled. It seemed to go on forever, down, and down, and down into nothingness. "The only thing we can do now is to stick close together and keep our eyes peeled for more booby traps and writing on the wall."

Chapter 27
✿ A Basket Case ✿

Cal and Ruben had tried to go in through the keep's front doors, but the guards there had barred the way, telling them that only those with an invite were allowed in.

"But we are squires of Sir Stanton of House Sprig," Cal had argued, "and we must find him!"

"You are squires you say?" the guard had asked.

"Yes!" Cal had answered triumphantly.

"Then I know you don't have an invitation," the guard had thrown in their faces.

Defeated, Cal and Ruben had left the front steps of the keep to formulate a plan.

Now they made their way to the deserted gardens, and sat beneath a large tree in the shade to discuss strategy. It was strange for Cal, having Ruben work with him instead of bullying him, and Cal wasn't too sure if he should get comfortable with the situation in case things went back the way they had been before. For now though, Cal was happy to have the older boy on his side.

"We need to find a way inside, but how?" Ruben wracked his brain for an idea.

"Why can't we just go in through the servant's entrance?" Cal asked.

"The palace has a set of servants like we do back at the manor. We would be recognized as not belonging there, especially with the doors being watched," Ruben explained.

"But we have to get in," Cal insisted, "Who knows where this will lead? The queen might even be in danger. We have to let someone know!"

"If it's that dire, you can come in with me," A pretty voice offered from above.

Cal looked up and when he saw the shapely green eyes staring down at him, his heart felt like it flipped once in his chest. *It's the girl with the apples,* Cal realized. He began to take more notice of where they were sitting. They had picked a seat among a small orchard of apple trees. There was a rustling of leaves and snapping of twigs as the girl began to descend. She jumped out of the tree when she got to the lowest branch, and hit the ground beside them with a thud.

She carefully spilled an armload of apples into a basket that had been placed on the other side of the tree. She heaved the basket up by the handles, and came around the tree to meet them. Cal had risen at the sound of her descending *thud*, and had quickly brushed off his clothes and smoothed his hair.

"I am Calen, squire to Sir Stanton of House Sprig," he said proudly and bowing to her. Cal heard a throat clear behind him. "And this is Ruben."

"Also a squire for House Sprig," the older boy added, sticking out his hand to clasp hers. She was too busy hefting the basket however, and he quickly let his hand drop. "And you are?"

"Beautiful," Cal exhaled dreamily. As soon as he realized that he had spoken out loud, he snapped to attention, and could feel his face go hot with embarrassment. "I mean...that is...er,"

The girl giggled and blushed, which only made her more becoming in Cal's opinion. "My name is Sabyn," she said, rescuing him.

Sabeen, what a beautiful name, he thought.

"I've been picking apples for days to collect enough for the feast this evening," she told them. "This wouldn't be the first time that I've gotten another servant to help me carry in the heavy baskets, they won't suspect a thing." She handed the basket she was holding to Ruben, who took the load easily. Then she got another basket and handed it to Cal, who struggled a bit with the weight. He wondered if he held the basket at the same angle Ruben did, if his muscles would bulge like that too. He adjusted the angle of the basket a few times, trying to make his arms look stronger, before she spoke. "Are you having trouble with that? Because I can carry it if you can't manage it."

"No, I'm fine!" He assured her, settling on the most comfortable way to hold his burden.

She nodded, her thick spill of tight brown ringlets bouncing with the motion. "As long as you're alright," she said as she found the last basket, "The ruse of you helping me wouldn't be very convincing if you can't lift the thing."

"Don't worry, I've got this," he reassured her, "It isn't that heavy." He was trying to sound macho, and had no idea if he was succeeding. He had never found talking to girls to be difficult before, why did he even care? She began to lead the way through the orchard toward the rear door to the keep. He found himself watching the hypnotic sway of her step, and deliberately looked toward the sky. The last thing he wanted was to be caught staring at her-

"Ah!" he yelped as he tripped over a rather large tree root.

She turned and her green eyes flashed at him. "Subtlety is not your forte, is it?" she hissed. "If you want this to work, you're going to have to try to be more careful," she scolded. "What were you looking at, anyway?"

"The sky," he answered back weakly. Ruben snickered behind him. *Great, I'm never going to hear the end of this.*

"Well, try to keep your eyes on what's before you!" she ordered.

He gulped. *Well, she had insisted.* Cal glued his eyes to the path. Now Ruben laughed out loud. She glared at him, and shook her head. Cal heard her huff the word "boys!" under her breath as she began to walk again.

They got to the servants' entrance, but the guards there were no friendlier than the ones at the front had been.

"Does your mother know that you're trailing a line of boys again, Sabyn?" the guard asked demeaningly. "You know what happened the last time."

Cal felt like punching him, but to her credit, Sabyn never lost her cool. Cal wondered if she was used to this treatment, and that made him want to hit the guard even more. *What's wrong with me?* he marvelled, completely mystified. *I'm not a violent person.*

"They're just helping me carry my apples, Henry," she said sweetly.

"Normally that would be ok," he talked down to her as if she was a dullard, "but today is the coronation, and nobody is allowed in without an invitation."

"No problem," she replied, "We'll just leave our baskets here, and you can do the job of a servant and carry them in for us. Don't worry, I won't tell any of the other guards that you left your post to work in the kitchen, I know how much that would bruise your ego." She said matter-of-factly. She turned to the boys behind her. "Alright boys, you can leave your baskets here, thanks for your help."

Cal was confused, this had not gone as planned, but he began to set down his basket.

"Fine, just make it quick," the surly guard allowed. "I really don't know where you find them,

Sabyn. Just make sure this is the last time this happens today."

"Yes, sir," she replied quickly, and breezed through the door before the guard could change his mind. Ruben and Cal followed, and soon found themselves in the kitchen, setting down their baskets near the station that was in full swing preparing desserts.

"You are amazing! I don't know how we'll ever thank you," Cal revelled at their small victory. He hadn't realized that he had taken her hands in his until she gave them a gentle squeeze.

"Oh, I'm sure you'll find a way," she said, looking demure. "You know, there's going to be a dance tonight after the feast," she reminded him expectantly.

"Only if we get to the queen in time," he reminded her, the urgency returning to his voice. "Now, how do we get to the throne room?"

Chapter 28
☼ Wet Behind the Ears ☼

It wasn't long before Lazelan felt like he was doing too much work to be simply walking down a hall.

"Do you feel that?" Lazelan asked the others.

"Yes, an inclined plane." Harmonium confirmed.

"What?" Wolfbane demanded crankily, "The only thing I feel is hot and tired, and ready for something to eat."

Lazelan unstopped his water skin and poured a small amount of the liquid on the smooth blocks underfoot. The water trickled away from them. He tried to tell the gnome that the flat ground had turned into a ramp that they were walking up, but Wolfbane wasn't listening. He was too busy sputtering over Lazelan's wasted water. "We're in the middle of a desert! What are you thinking? No, wait, we're not even in a desert, we're trapped in a *pyramid* in a desert. There is no chance of catching rain, or finding a cactus or-"

While Wolfbane had been ranting, Lazelan had cast a spell which had sucked a large amount of water droplets out of the air. He had held the rippling liquid orb above the gnome's head until now. *Sploosh*, Lazelan released the water all over his overheated friend. The mage wasn't worried about wasting it, he could cast a spell that would summon more a hundred times a day. If he didn't drain all of his energy, that was.

The sopping wet gnome stood with his arms slightly raised, dripping all over the floor. His face was a mask of shock. The water that fell from his clothing and armour created a little stream that flowed downhill, which illustrated Lazelan's point very neatly.

"We're walking uphill?" Wolfbane inquired calmly.

"Yes," Lazelan replied. "Now we really have to watch out for traps. What goes up, must come down." he reasoned. The three of them began to move again, taking more care to check the walls and floors for cracks or holes that might be a sign of something dangerous lying in wait.

The incline grew steeper, until it plateaued. At the top was another mirror, which shone its light on a new message carved into a new brick:

The flat space at the top of the ramp was very unusual. As they got closer, Lazelan could see that the bit of flat floor wasn't very big, and it gave way to water. The water was so calm it looked like shimmering glass, and beyond that was another wall. It appeared to be a dead end.

The carvings in this brick were much smaller than the last. In order to see the block well enough to read the inscription, they'd have to cram themselves up onto the little bit of floor. *It might not be that bad,* Lazelan reckoned, *Wolfbane can't read the script anyway, so he can stay down on the ramp. In fact, only one of us really has to fit in the space.*

"There is only room for one reader," he told Harmonium. The older mage stepped forward, but Lazelan grabbed his arm to halt him. "Be careful. I will watch the water in case something comes out of it for us.

"What are the chances of that happening?" Wolfbane asked as he eyed the water mistrustfully.

"The last time we found an inscription, there was a trap. It stands to reason that the closer we get, the more elaborate the traps will become." Harmonium reported. "This is often the way of secret societies." He stepped forward up onto the flat piece of floor to read the message there on the wall, and instantly there was a succession of clicking noises, and the hall itself began to move. The wall that marked the dead end past the watery floor began to press towards them, skimming across the water, and forcing some of it to start spilling back down the ramp over Lazelan's and Wolfbane's feet.

"Read quickly!" Lazelan urged, as the wall moved closer and more water poured down the ramp they were standing on. Harmonium quickly read the riddle:

"Ey jaxa jo failiyat bod Ey jaxaraux jo failatiyat,
Ey jaxa jo jehixiyat bod raux tatoa hixiyat,
Ey taja yesra snita tati Tay masnift sor,
Est tati Ey tast fallotiyat, Tay tajaraux isa so liyet fue."

Lazelan called out the words in the common tongue spoken by most people of the land so Wolfbane could understand.

"I can be held but I can't be clutched,
I can be felt, but not really touched.
I will come quickly if you run away,
And if I am stopped, you won't see the next day."

The wall continued to move steadily, and had reached the halfway point across what had been the watery floor. The liquid was pouring down the ramp now, and it made it hard for Lazelan to keep his footing. The stone under foot was beginning to get slick and hard to stand on without falling.

"I was going to say *honor*, but that only fits with the first part of the riddle." Wolfbane said. He began hitting his forehead with the palm of his hand, saying "think, think, think!"

The wall was closing in, in six short feet, it would reach where they stood. Lazelan suspected they would all end up being forced back down the ramp with the torrent of water that was getting stronger with every inch. *The water must be pretty deep,* he figured.

"It is *breath*," Harmonium concluded.

Lazelan understood what the message meant. He just hoped there was nothing dangerous in the water after all.

"Follow me, quickly!" Lazelan commanded. He took a deep breath, ran up the path past Harmonium, and plunged into the water. He prepared for the impact of hitting the moving wall under the water's surface, but no impact came. *It's only just skimming the water,* he realized. The water was icy cold, probably kept that way by magic, and after the hot air of the desert, his body started to go into hypothermic shock. He forced his seizing muscles to swim down, to give his friends room to follow. He could see a glowing light many feet below him, and he struggled to swim to that.

He heard sounds behind him that told him that his friends had followed, but there was a jarring noise, followed by a squealing and then a loud *clank*. Something heavy sunk rapidly past him in a shroud of bubbles. Lazelan kept moving. His ears became painful as he swam lower and lower. He was finding it harder and harder to make his muscles do what he wanted. They just didn't seem to want to move. He released some of his precious air to allow himself to sink faster.

As he neared the bottom, he saw the armoured Wolfbane there, rescuing his broken dagger from amid a bunch of stone spheres that littered the ground. *He must have just made it through,* Lazelan realized. *His dagger got caught, that's what the sound was, his dagger being snapped by the closing of the wall.*

The floor was made of polished tiles, like in a throne room, and in the centre, was a giant opened pot or urn. From around the edges of the tile it was set on, came the yellow light Lazelan had been following. They looked at the walls around them, but there were no clues as to what their next step should be. At least they seemed to be alone in what appeared to be a square room, with no monsters to attack them, at least not yet. Lazelan scanned the walls again and didn't see any kind of door or other way out. His lungs began to burn. He wouldn't be able to hold his breath much longer. As he watched his friends do nothing but survey their surroundings, he feared that he had led them all into what might become a watery grave.

Chapter 29
✿ A Royal Scandal ✿

As they left the kitchen and made their way down the corridor to the throne room, Cal noted that barely a soul could be seen or heard. The coronation was concluding, and everyone was pent up behind the oak doors, watching.   From the sudden sound of cheers and clapping, the ceremony had gone off without a hitch. Cal and Ruben waited outside the throne room, listening to the applause and waiting for people to begin pouring out through the hallway. The heavy oak doors blew open and the king and queen brushed past them and rushed down the hall. The new king was walking quickly, as if on a mission. Cal hadn't missed the beaming smile on the king's face. The queen trailed after, although she appeared to be trying to keep up with him.

"Oslan, slow down!" the queen cried in a hushed voice as she fell behind again, "I must talk to you, it's important!"

"Perhaps we should wait until they're not so busy?" Cal asked Ruben as they started to follow after the royal couple.

"They're rulers, if you want to wait until they're no longer busy, I'm afraid you'll have to tell them our news at their funerals, and then it will be too late." Ruben argued.

Cal followed the royal couple with his eyes as they got farther and farther away from the two squires. All of a sudden, the king stopped and the queen ploughed right into the back of him. Cal watched as the king turned and caught the queen before she could fall from the impact. They appeared to be sharing a moment, and Cal really didn't want to interrupt, but it had to be done. A group of nobles passed by and interrupted the couple long enough to bow to them and congratulate them. Then, they moved on and the king and queen exchanged a few more words before beginning to walk arm in arm at a much slower pace.

"Come on, now's our chance," he told Ruben. The boys raced up the hall with quick walking steps to catch them. "Excuse me, Your Majesties!" Cal called to catch their attention.

Two knights that Cal hadn't noticed before stepped forward from against the wall, intercepting them as they neared the royal couple. Cal's stomach jumped up into his throat, and he stopped short. His heart began to pound loudly in his ears, and he could feel his hands break out in a clammy sweat. *Why do I feel like a criminal getting caught?* He tried to fathom, *we are here to help them*. Cal didn't like confrontation, and he hated to be made to feel like he was doing something wrong. He realized he was starting to feel guilty. He tried to reason it out and bury the feeling inside.

The newly crowned king and queen turned toward them, and Cal was surprised to note that the king couldn't have been even as old as Ruben. Cal wouldn't get to become a knight until he was around twenty-one, and he couldn't imagine having the responsibilities of running a whole kingdom at a younger age. He regretted having to add to the weight that the king's shoulders were bearing, but he knew the king and queen needed to know that a plot was afoot.

Cal and Ruben bowed low to Oslan and Aylan. "We have some information that we think you should hear," Ruben said.

"Is there somewhere private where we can talk?" Cal asked, eyeing the closest guard.

The king looked to the queen, and Cal could

tell there was some kind of silent conversation passing between them.

"What is this concerning?" She asked.

"We have uncovered a plot of sorts, but we're not sure how it will play out. All we can tell you right now, is that we fear that some danger may befall the queen." Ruben answered.

Oslan waived the guards back, and they retreated to their original posts.

"There is more," Cal assured them.

"Let us go to the war room," Oslan replied, on a day like today, we should find some privacy there."

A few minutes later, the two boys were sitting across from the king and queen at the largest table that Cal had ever seen. One end of the table was littered with rolled up maps and scrolls, and behind the king and queen, hung a huge tapestry on the wall. The weaver had been very skilled. It was woven in great detail, and showed each estate in the kingdom. Each manor was depicted with a flag bearing the house's name and coat of arms. The farms were all present as well, as were each of the peasants' domiciles; however they were marked by a simple hut, or a deeper shade of green to signify rich pasture land. With the whole kingdom laid out like that, taking up nearly an entire wall, Cal felt very small.

"Now, how is it that you feel that my wife is in danger?" Oslan demanded, planting his hands on the table before him. The queen gently took his hand.

"Peace, dear, they have come to us as friends," she soothed him. "Tell us what you know." She asked of the squires.

Cal waited for Ruben to start, after all, he'd been doing most of the talking so far. It made sense, he was the older boy at almost twenty. Any information they had would sound more plausible coming from an adult. When the air was met with silence, he saw the king and queen turn their attention to him. His hands that had dried, broke out in a sweat once more. He studied the grain of wood in the heavy table, trying to find the best words to use. He didn't want to gush like a child, he needed them to believe him, and he found he didn't really know where to start. All of this information was new to him too.

"I guess it all started when I began having trouble sleeping," he started. The king cut him off.

"How does that have anything to do with the queen?" he inquired. "This is a very big day for us, and we have things to attend to. Spit it out, boy!"

Cal heard a rustle of fabric come from under the table, followed by a look of pain and surprise on the king's previously stern face. Now he looked confused, and peered for a moment at the queen incredulously. She returned an expression of complete innocence, with raised eyebrows as if to say "Whatever can be the matter, dear?" Another of those silent conversations followed, and the king sat down. He gave his attention back to Cal, and politely asked the boy to continue, if he would.

Cal thought he could kiss the queen right then, and knew he had made the right decision to come to help protect her. She was a gem.

"Well, Your Highnesses, there is a man, Master Augden Zalice, who is a herbologist like the queen..."

He tried to keep it short and succinct, and Cal thought in the end, that he had done a pretty good job of it. He told them about Master Zalice's visits at bed time, and his sleeping draughts that never seemed to work. He explained about finding the strange box that he had never seen before, mixed in amongst his things. He told them about the man strangely showing up at the castle, and his persistence in wanting to help Cal sleep.

Ruben added what he knew about the night that he had seen Cal break into the inn, and the items that had shown up in Cal's pouch. He finished by pulling out the letter that he and Ruben had found. He unfolded it for the king and queen, holding it flat on the table for them to read.

"It's a petition?" Aylan asked.

"It's a petition," Oslan echoed, "One that requests that none other than Augden Zalice be appointed as the court's official herbologist. Luckily, it's not yet complete."

"But Oslan, that's silly, we don't need a herbologist. I might be your mage now, but I can still see to the nobles' ailments. In fact, I've become so capable with the help of magic, that I have been able to make a stock pile of tinctures and salves ahead of time for various illnesses. This has to be some mistake. He can't really think to replace me, can he?"

The queen looked a bit panicked, and for that, Cal felt bad. She hadn't even realized the worst of it yet.

"The petition, as things stand now, is useless. You are our herbologist," Oslan reassured her, "and this can't replace you. Normally, in the event that a court appointed official is removed from office, becomes too ill to see to his duties, or dies, the council will meet to discuss who will fill the empty position. A petition bearing the seal of ten prominent nobles, two of which must sit on the council, can quicken those discussions by acting as a pre-recorded vote." He explained. "There are only eight seals stamped here, he is short by two."

"But I feel fine, and I have never heard of this Augden Zalice. I would think that if all of these nobles were willing to affix their seals to this letter, he would be someone of note." she reasoned.

"The nobles never saw the petition," Ruben interjected. "Zalice has been hypnotizing Cal into doing his dirty work for him. The sleeping draughts are a cover-up. Cal has been operating in a trance during the night to procure the imprints the herbologist needs. That is why Cal is constantly tired, and it's no wonder why. I even saw Cal perform feats I'd never give him credit for being able to do normally. When I went to confront him for myself, he didn't come to his senses right away, and when he did, he was bewildered. He didn't even know where he was." Ruben explained emphatically. "That is how I know that my fellow squire is innocent in all of this."

Ruben put his hand on Cal's closest shoulder to show his support, and Cal felt a deep sense of bewilderment. *Master Zalice has used me for treachery, and Ruben of all people stands by my side? Has the whole world gone mad?* he pondered.

The queen looked taken aback. "What are we to do with this information, Oslan? With me around, this petition has no place."

"Which is why we thought you might be in danger," Cal pointed out. "We figure he must be planning something sinister to make his plan succeed."

"But this is over, we have the scroll now," She decided.

"Yes and no." Oslan told her. "We have the scroll, which may stop him, and may make him go into hiding to avoid punishment for his crimes. But he has done some heinous things here, the least of which is pulling this young boy into a world of treachery and danger. Moreover, the nobles need to feel safe here, and he could be plotting against us. We could be looking at an act of treason. I want the people of my kingdom to know that when they wake in the morning, all will still be as they left it."

Cal dropped his gaze to the table top. He couldn't face his king and queen right now, he felt too guilty. Even though he knew he would never have chosen to enter those nobles' rooms under the cover of night if the choice had been left to him, he had committed the acts on Master Zalice's behalf. Never before had he felt so much like a lost little boy. He felt used and weak.

Oslan stood, and read the parchment again. He began tapping the empty spot for the two missing seals with his knuckle as he thought.

"We can't prove that he has a direct connection to the petition. We have to tie him to it somehow. He still has two signatures to get, and they must belong to our council members." Oslan began to pace back and forth along his side of the table, with one arm crossed through the other, and the second hand grasping his chin. He began mumbling to himself, and would occasionally shake his head.

"Coming to the palace would give him the perfect opportunity to get the two seals from the council members, which he hasn't done yet. But time is running out for him. In a day or two, all of the visitors that have come for the coronation will have gone, and his presence will be noted if he lingers here." He continued pacing, speeding up slightly. "I've got it!" he exclaimed. He re-folded the parchment, and handed it back to Cal. "This is what we're going to do."

Chapter 30
✿ In the Drink ✿

Lazelan watched as Wolfbane picked up one of the alabaster orbs, swam close to a wall, and attempted to throw the orb at it. It clacked off the wall and landed with a sound like cracking rock. Lazelan wasn't sure what Wolfbane had been trying to do, but it was obvious that nothing had changed.

Lazelan's lungs were burning intensely. He was going to need air soon, but the water appeared to go right to the ceiling now, affording them no room to breathe. He felt himself start to panic and his mind began running in useless circles like a rat in a cage. He swam to the nearest wall of the almost completely square room. He began to frantically run his fingers down each wall, searching for any cracks that might denote a way out. He found nothing, no seam, crack, or blemish on the smoothly polished stone walls. The answer had to lie with the urn or one of the stones. His lungs felt like they would explode. He couldn't hold his breath any longer, he needed some release. He let a small amount of air escape his lips, and instantly felt a small amount of relief. This was paired with regret as he watched the air escape upward.

He tried to move toward the urn and staggered. His vision was growing dark and blurrier than the water should be the cause of. He rubbed his eyes, not that it did much good. He could feel his consciousness passing away from him, like one of Magdolyn's fleeting glances when she had met him for the first time. Like her glances though, it kept returning. Step by heavy step, he dragged his legs forward. He saw Harmonium bring his hands together, and watched as a hot white light appeared between them.

Lazelan tried to focus his mind back on his target, he forced his leaden right foot to move another step. On the other side of the room, Wolfbane fell, and sunk quickly to the floor in a great flurry of bubbles that escaped his lungs. Lazelan found it almost impossible to think. His world was growing grey, and began to slide sideways as he took his last step. His own air, burning like hot fire in his chest, burst out of him and floated away. *Crack*, he felt a sharp pain slash across his side as he landed on the urn and rolled off it to the floor. He had probably broken a couple of ribs in that fall.

He watched from his sideways vantage point, as Harmoniums hands parted, revealing a small bubble of air between them. Tiny particles of air flew through the water, and joined the bubble, helping it grow larger and larger. Harmonium fell to his knees, and blinked hard. His eyebrows knit together in a final feat of concentration, and he brought the bubble to his lips. *What a good idea,* Lazelan had time to remark as he slid into unconsciousness.

*　　*　　*

Augden sat nursing his brew as he waited for a plate of supper to be brought to his table. He was sitting in the Rampaging Old Bear's tavern, watching the light start to wane outside. He had waited impatiently all day, going out of his mind with panic over the fact that Calen had not returned the night before with the pouch containing his scroll and box. Previously, he had made the boy hide it among his own things until Augden could collect it, but after the boy had accidently stumbled across it, the herbologist didn't want to risk it being discovered again.

Today while he waited, he had inconspicuously followed Lady Danelyn, and had taken note that the signet ring was once again upon her finger. Good, that part of the lad's quest had not gone awry then, so what had? The instructions had been quite clear, he had thought. It wouldn't be long now though, before he could go and see for himself. He would take another one of his faux sleeping draughts to the boy and could check for himself what state his pouch was in.

A serving wench wearing a dark green dress and white apron brought a steaming bowl of pottage, a goblet of spiced mead, and some bread. He tipped a large spoonful back into his mouth, and almost instantly spat it back into his bowl as it seared his tongue. He gulped the mead greedily, trying to cool the burning in his mouth. The room temperature drink didn't do much to quell the burning, but it was better than nothing. He drained the cup and asked for another. When she went, he chastised himself for causing a scene. He had wanted to go unnoticed. Hopefully he would be forgotten by anyone that might have noticed him. He shifted his gaze around the room. He didn't think any had.

He took his time finishing his food, if it could be called that. In an establishment like this, the cook had skimped. This pottage was thin and contained no meat. Augden had expected more than some cabbage and a few leeks and onions. *If I had wanted that, I could have stayed at home*, he grumbled. He set down his spoon, and finished off his spiced wine. *It's finally time to see to the boy,* he decided. He rechecked his bag to see that he had remembered to pack one of the sleeping potions he had made for Cal. It was there. He took hold of his walking stick and hobbled out the door to find out what had happened to Calen the night before.

* * *

Cal and Ruben had made a plan of sorts. The king had asked the younger squire if he would be willing to be hypnotized again. Cal hadn't liked the idea, but Ruben had assured him that he would stay awake and watch over him. Master Zalice might not go through with it if he found Ruben to be awake, so Ruben was to appear to be asleep already, as he had been the prior night. He could lay awake and listen to the instructions given to Cal when the herbologist put him into a trance. Ruben was then charged with relaying the message of which council member would be the next target. After delivering the message, he would go to the quarters of the council member in question to await Cal's arrival.

For their part, the king and queen had alerted the council members as to the possible conspiracy, and had told them to instruct their servants not to hurt the boy if he was caught in the act. They were to let the situation play out, and report back to the king or queen what they had seen. This would help corroborate the squires' accusations against Augden Zalice. Then all they would have to do would be to search the herbologist's belongings and hopefully find the letter amongst his things.

Chapter 31
☼ That Sinking Sensation ☼

Lazelan slowly came to. His body had a queer weightless quality to it, and he was cold all over, like when he swam in the creek near his house. His memory came flooding back, including his thoughts right before he had blacked out. His vision was blurry under the water, but as far as he could tell, the scenery hadn't changed. He was still submerged in the underwater room, but miraculously, he could breathe. *Thank all that is bright*, he thought with relief. Harmonium knelt before him, holding his bubble of air to Lazelan's mouth and nose. The young mage's ribs ached. He was still lying beside the urn in an uncomfortable position. He drew in a deep breath, and gritted his teeth at the sharp pain in his ribs that came as he did. He saw the bubble grow slightly smaller as he inhaled, and pointed at the gnome's form that lay not too far away on the floor.

Harmonium pulled away the life-saving oxygen and took a deep breath of air for himself as he brought the bubble to their other fallen friend.

Lazelan worked to stand up using the edge of the urn for support. When he did, he felt it shift under his weight and things were set into motion all at once. The crack of light around the edges of the tile that housed the urn seemed to glow slightly brighter. It had sunken into the floor on the side that his hand held, to make an uneven crack like a door that had been left ajar. There was a great flurry of bubbles which raced toward the ceiling, and inert particles in the water near that tile began to race toward the glow.

Lazelan felt excitement and hope bloom inside him as he realized there was a way they may be able to escape this predicament. *The water is being released!* Lazelan finished standing and released the urn. It shifted again and the glowing space lessened, the light dimmed, and the water once again became stagnant. Panic started to creep in as he looked up and saw that there was not yet enough room between the ceiling and water to breathe. Harmonium's solution worked, but there was only so much oxygen in the water. It would run out. He looked around again at the orbs on the floor, and the idea enlightened him like a light coming on in an attic.

He felt around for one of the stone orbs that littered the floor everywhere. Stubbing the tips of his fingers against one, he grabbed it. He sat like that for a few precious seconds as his body continued to use up the air in his lungs. He was afraid to lift the orb off the ground. So many things had been a trap so far in this place, and he didn't want to set off another one. He thought he knew the answer, but of course, it wasn't certain. He considered the consequences of leaving the orb where it was, and the possibility of making enough space to breathe. His lungs once again began to scream for air, and he alleviated the feeling momentarily by letting a rivulet of bubbles escape his lips.

He made the choice and lifted the stone orb easily in one hand. He looked around, but nothing seemed to be happening. He listened intently, but no sound signaling the movement of a trap came. He relaxed a bit, but started moving the orb through the water. He examined it, and found it was rather heavy for its size, and had been polished smooth. In fact, Lazelan's fingers did not detect a chip or crack in its surface at all. He gently laid it in the urn.

He had expected to see the space around the tile grow bigger, and the glow to re-appear brighter.

It did, but on a much smaller scale than before. Out of the fissure flew a few rogue bubbles that flitted upward in a tiny stream of air. He could see the water starting to seep through the crack that had been ever so slightly spread by the weight of the stone in the urn. He looked at his companions, now both on their feet, and motioned for them to add more.

Harmonium and Wolfbane understood at once, and after taking one last new breath from Harmonium's air-filled bubble, they began gathering as many of the round stones as they could carry.

With each new polished orb, the weight in the urn grew, spreading the glowing gap more and more as the tile it was standing on sunk down into the floor. The glowing bright light was gaining an intensity that made it hard to look at. Lazelan could now feel the pull of the water as it drained out of the room, creating its own dangerous sucking current. He watched as some of the remaining balls began to roll with the force of the water towards the gaping space between the tiles. The urn was overflowing with the mound of stones now, and had sunken so far into the floor that the lip of the urn was almost level with the other tiles on the ground.

The dropping water level in the room had come down about half way. A whirl pool had begun and a tornado-like funnel of water circled round and round and down towards the gap in the floor. Lazelan wasn't sure that his rather weak upper body strength could withstand the current, but Harmonium's air bubble was gone. He had let it go when they had started to gather the stones. But Lazelan once again needed to breathe. He pushed off the bottom with his sandaled feet, and swam upwards with all his might to get a new breath of hot desert air.

He had just broken the surface long enough to gasp in a lungful of air, when the current became more than he could handle. Lazelan began sinking against his will, fast. His exhausted legs kicked, and he stroked with his long arms but by no means did he have an athletic body type. His wiry frame sunk like a ship taking on water.

His two companions were trying to overcome the current in their own ways. Wolfbane had backed up against one wall and had braced his feet against the pull. It would be hard for the water to get between him and the wall to force him forward. For Harmonium's part, now with ample air in the room, he had created a giant bubble of air big enough to encase him completely. The water whooshed by the bubble, gliding easily around its round surface, finding nothing to grab onto. Harmonium was concentrating hard now though. Lazelan could see the struggle etched on his face. Harmonium had to keep the bubble of air, whose nature it was to float upwards, down where the mage was to protect himself. The bigger the bubble, the bigger the pull it would have.

As Lazelan was pulled into the whirlpool, he felt himself moving faster, his body being forced to whip around. He stopped fighting it. He had reached his physical limit and his muscles felt like the congealed fat from a piece of meat, all jiggling jelly. As he drew closer to the space the water was funnelling out of, he tried to aim his feet so that they landed on opposite sides of the lip of the urn to stop himself from getting lodged in the crack. One sandaled toe touched down, then the other, and the urn dropped nearly a foot, down into the hole with his weight. He pushed off with his legs as the urn slid sideways under the tile that had been next to it on the floor. The current of the whirlpool became grander as the tile and urn were no longer there to stem the flow of water. The rushing liquid slammed him into the wall, dragging him along for a few feet as it did. His fingertips scrabbled for anything he could get a hold of to stop himself as he fell to the ground. All he got for his trouble were a few grabbed and discarded stone orbs. A terrifying sucking and gurgling sound began to come from the hole the water was disappearing through as it gushed out of the room faster and faster.

The glow coming from the hole was now blinding as something blazed from underneath. Lazelan's hands and knees began to find purchase on the smooth ground as he gradually felt his weight return to him. A sense of relief washed over him as he realized that the water was low enough now that he had to support himself. Finally, his head broke the surface. The water level sunk lower and lower as it disappeared. A few moments later, the gargling sound stopped and the last few inches of water leaked out through the hole.

Chapter 32
☼ On a Roll ☼

Cal and Ruben had already changed out of their tunics, into their bedclothes and had bedded down for the night. Cal lay awake in the dim glow of their single candle, wondering if maybe Master Zalice wasn't going to come. If truth be told, a part of him hoped the herbologist wouldn't show.

Then the familiar *click-step, click-step,* of Master Zalice walking with his stick grew clearer as the man drew near their quarters. Ruben nodded at Calen in reassurance, and pulled his own covers up high to obscure most of his face.

"Master Zalice, is that you?" Call called out, already dreading the answer he knew would come.

"Yes, it is, my child, may I come in?" the man replied expectantly.

Cal's skin crawled. He felt dirty at the thought of what he knew was coming. He was about to offer his mind up to this man again, and the herbologist was going to make him commit more illegal acts. These were not the deeds of a gentleman. *How can I ever become a knight knowing about these breaches that I have committed?* Cal's mind questioned. The only reason that he spoke the words he said next was because it was his duty to obey the king and queen. Therefore, he must at least attempt to follow the king's plan, whether he agreed with it or not. He answered the herbologist's knock.

"Then enter, please, for I feel I might need your help tonight." the boy allowed.

The herbologist entered with his staff and sack, and came to sit in his familiar place at the end of Cal's bed. Did he look suspicious? Cal couldn't tell. Cal didn't lie as a rule, and he honestly wasn't sure he'd be able to do it convincingly. If he couldn't get Master Zalice to give him another sleeping draught, it would sink the whole plan though like a ship in a storm. A part of Cal just wanted to grab the front of the man's robes and scream at the man for invading his mind and for using him. The worst part was in knowing that he had to allow the herbologist to do it again.

"What is it that you need my help with, boy?" Master Zalice asked. He seemed to be acting cautious.

"Last night I woke too soon," Cal began. Master Zalice sat up quickly, leaned toward him and planted a hand on the bed between them. His eyes seemed to bore into Cal's soul.

"And what happened?" the vial man asked him, full of concern.

"Nightmares," Cal spat out after a brief hesitation, "I had awful nightmares. I think I need a stronger draught tonight, if you have one."

Master Zalice leaned back. He seemed satisfied and relieved. Cal felt sick. *You never cared about me,* Cal yelled in his mind, *you just cared about not getting caught.* He tried his hardest not to show what he was feeling, and covered it up with what he hoped was a convincing yawn. He set his features in a mask of tiredness, but he dreaded what was coming next.

When they had formed the plan, Cal hadn't been sure he would be able to be put into a trance again. The queen had told him that in order for that to happen, one had to give over their mind willingly, and Cal no longer trusted the man. The queen had pointed out that if Cal was unable to be put under, Master Zalice might be desperate enough to try controlling someone else, or might end up harming someone. As a result, Cal was determined to try to follow the man's directions completely. He knew Ruben was standing by to keep him safe, and it was the only way to catch this scoundrel in the act.

Master Zalice handed him the bottle containing the familiar purple liquid, and got ready with his shining coin. Without taking his eyes off the man, Cal unstopped the bottle's cork with his teeth and spat it onto the bed. He drank down the mixture, grimacing at the rotten taste flooding his mouth, and once again wondered what exactly he was putting into his body. He handed the bottle back to the herbologist, and only then dropped his eyes to find the cork that lay on his blanket.

As he picked it up and handed it back, he silently reminded himself how important it was to follow through with the plan. He steadied himself and prepared himself to give over control of his mind. The coin started its usual rolling and dipping over the backs of Master Zalice's fingers.

Unsurprisingly, some of the amazement of the act was now lost on Cal, like the time his uncle had wowed him as a young boy by pulling a coin out of his ear. His uncle's feat had seemed impossible, until Cal had seen him do again to his cousin. This time, Cal had been watching from the other side, and saw how the trick had been performed. The magic in the act had evaporated, and had seemed completely unimpressive from then on.

Still, Cal couldn't let Master Zalice know that he could see right through his act. Cal buckled down and allowed himself to become mesmerized by the rhythmic movement and flash of the silver in the candlelight. His eyelids grew heavier and heavier until he could hold them up no longer.

Chapter 33
☼ Taking the Fall ☼

Lazelan, Harmonium, and Wolfbane stood dripping into the puddles left on the slick floor. The light blazing out of the slot left from the missing tile was growing steadily hotter. Lazelan could see the small droplets of water still dangling from the edge of the floor turn into tendrils of steam as they let go and fell down toward light. The heat that was radiating from the source had made the temperature in the room rise, and Lazelan took note that the sleeve closest the square was even beginning to dry.

"What now?" Wolfbane asked, "There's no door."

"No," Lazelan agreed. He had already come to that conclusion. The walls were bare, and only a couple of orbs were left lying on the ground here and there. There seemed to be nothing else in the room except for his party of friends. He edged closer to the hole in the ground and attempted to brave the wave of heat that scalded his sunburned face. He wanted to get a look at what was below the floor.

He gasped as he peered into the hole at what he saw there. The heat radiating upwards filled his lungs with the feeling of burning fire. He stepped back quickly, coughing raggedly at the assault on his tired and already aching body.

"What is it?" Wolfbane asked excitedly, and took a few steps toward the hole so he could see into the heat-filled void.

"Whoa!" He exclaimed as he threw his arms up to shield his face, and squinted against the harsh light.

"Are we meant to take that?" Lazelan wondered out loud.

"Seems like we might have to," Wolfbane

decided, "but do either of you have any *bright* ideas as to how we can get it out?"

"With magic," Harmonium declared, ignoring the pun. He held his hand toward the hole in the floor and called the item to him in Almatrae. The light intensified as it began to pass up into the room they occupied. It was a curved sword and although the hilt looked to be fairly normal, the blade itself was ablaze. Harmonium brought the scimitar up until it cleared the floor completely, and then a series of clicks and clacks made Lazelan's blood run cold.

As one wall began to trundle slowly toward them, new tile slid up to block the hole in the floor from underneath. There was a beautifully carved boarder inside the edges of the tile, which bore an inscription within it. Lazelan began to read out loud automatically

"*Ey taja tramas xilox jus Ey falt,*
Sult nula hafae fari,
So nol trayt tajas yesra est gallot,
Liyat Ey taja saira sultir box."

Harmonium dropped his spell in order to shift his concentration to the new key to their escape. With no spell keeping it aloft, the fine sword plummeted toward the ground. The mage repeated the words, this time in the common language for the gnome:

> *"I'll grow colder till I pass,*
> *One of siblings four,*
> *The other three shall come and go,*
> *Then I'll return once more."*

Unfortunately, the recitation was all for naught. Wolfbane, with eyes only for the flaming treasure, launched himself through the air to intercept the fiery scimitar before it could hit the floor. The gnome's outstretched fingers closed around the weapon's hilt, and the small man screamed. Lazelan heard the immediate sizzle and smelled the meaty odour of the gnome's flesh burning as the searing hilt branded his tiny hand.

As Wolfbane howled in pain, Lazelan was blinded by a flash of white light that blew outward from the hilt. He couldn't see. It was as if someone had dropped a white veil over the world. He staggered and felt disoriented, but he could still hear the stone wall moving on some unseen track, followed by the sound of Wolfbane and his gear landing and sliding a short distance across the floor.

"Fall down," Wolfbane shouted, "quickly, both of you!"

Lazelan turned his head toward the sound of the gnome's voice. He had heard the desperation in his friend's command, and did not waste any time. He dropped to his stomach and rested prone on the floor, shutting his eyes to better focus on what his other senses were telling him. He realized that his friend had stopped screaming, and crawled on his belly toward the sound of his ally's voice. The clacking of the wall's gears continuing to move and the scraping of one wall against the other as it drew ever closer hadn't slowed.

"We have to figure out the riddle, or we'll be squashed!" Lazelan called out desperately, there's still no way out." He tried opening his eyes, but all he saw were blurs of colours, shadows and lights. His eyes stung, and they didn't seem able to focus. The sound of the wall drew nearer. Soon they would have to move or be flattened.

"Listen to the ground!" Harmonium instructed from close by.

Lazelan pressed his ear to the cool wet tile, but heard nothing but the dampened noises of the same gears turning to operate the trap.

"I hear noth-" Lazelan began, but was cut off by his old master.

"Listen carefully!" the old man instructed in a deceivingly younger, yet forceful voice. So Lazelan tried harder to hear what he had missed. After a few valuable seconds longer, seconds that seemed to stretch out like eons, he still could only hear the wall moving closer.

We're done, he realized then that they had failed. Endalwynndale so desperately needed the *Almatraek Bright,* but now he knew he wouldn't be the one to find it. Their quest was at an end, and he felt as though they had only just begun. They needed a way out, but he couldn't even remember the lines of the riddle in order to solve it, and he couldn't see well enough to go read it again. He thought about grabbing the urn so they could prop it up against one wall to create a safe space for them by holding back the other. But the urn was gone, and he wasn't sure if it would have withstood the pressure of the moving wall anyway. *Perhaps we could climb down the hole that the urn had disappeared into.* He thought that might work. *Was that what the riddle had been about? Would it get the stone to open for us again before we get squashed like a leaf in a mortar and pestle?*

The clacking was growing louder, the scraping of the wall closer. He thought that must be it. He blinked his eyes forcefully, trying to clear the blur, but it didn't help. His eyes were still useless. He squeezed them shut and felt helpless to save them. He considered casting a spell to hold apart the walls, like a bubble of safety, but he knew it would only delay the inevitable. The spell would only work as long as he could keep it up, and with the mechanical wall pressing against it, his energy would eventually drain away into the spell until it winked out. After the ordeal of working underwater, taxing his lungs, and swimming against the forceful current, he was all but exhausted. His spell wouldn't last very long. He supposed that had been the point of the water in the room, to tire out a mage that might have made it that far.

The scraping grew louder still, and his stomach turned with fear. Sorrow crept into his heart in those last few moments. He felt responsible for the imminent deaths of his master and his new friend. He knew Harmonium wouldn't blame him. The older mage believed in taking responsibility for one's choices and it had been his choice to come. But he wondered if Wolfbane would feel the same way. *Is he laying there wishing me ill right now?* he pondered.

The wall was close, the scraping and clacking filled his ears. It occurred to him that no one knew where their quest had taken them. He filled his mind with comforting thoughts of his wife, and was thankful that Maggie would never have to know how he had died.

Chapter 34
☼ A Helping Hand ☼

As soon as the boy was under, Augden stopped talking to him. He was now free to search through Cal's things for his missing pouch and box.

Leaving the boy in the trance, he dropped his silver coin back into his pouch and stood. He went to the familiar trunk which held the boy's clothes and possessions, and attempted to kneel down in front of it. His bad leg protested painfully and he bit off a scream so as not to wake the sleeping squire in the other bed. He was left half kneeling and half crouching awkwardly in front of the wooden chest. He opened the lid and began carefully lifting the edges of garments to feel around for his things without upsetting the way the clothes were packed. It just wouldn't do to have the boy discover later that his things had been tampered with. That might break the bond of trust the boy had with him, and then he might be impossible to put under. Augden always liked to keep his options opened. That way, if one door was closed in your face, you could always escape out a window.

His fingers felt a rectangular lump the right size, and he knew he had found it. He grasped the box through the material of the pouch, and extracted them both together.

He hurriedly loosened the drawstring, and opened the mouth of the small sack. He pulled out the box and opened it to check its contents. *Everything is still here,* he admitted in relief. *My plan can move ahead tonight, but I may have to speed things along.*

He tried to get up to return to the boy, but found his knee wouldn't support his weight. He looked over to the child's bed. There was his helpful walking staff that he had left leaning against it just out of reach. He spoke to the boy, "When you hear the word *help*, you will help me up."

He wished the boy was close enough to touch. Augden wasn't sure how deeply the boy was under, and being able to touch his hand, shoulder or forehead could send him down deeper. This would ensure the boy really was completely under his control. *No matter, it still may work,* he reasoned. *Even if he isn't down deep enough to follow my suggestion, Cal is a good boy, and would do what I ask anyway. I will just have to elaborate then.*

"Help," he spoke the key word. The boy immediately threw off his covers, stood, walked over to the herbologist, and took his offered hand. He struggled and pulled the man up until he was set right on his feet. Cal dropped the man's hand and stood waiting for his next set of instructions. *Good, very good.*

Before this evening, Augden had only dared to make Cal visit one home on each of his excursions to attain the stamped seals that he required for his advancement. Tonight though, the boy would be visiting two. Last night had worried Augden. The not-knowing what had happened to his purse was almost worse than getting caught, and he wanted his things to be back in his own possession once and for all.

He spent the next few minutes talking to Cal, and planting suggestions into the boy's subconscious. When he was done, he sent the boy to sit for an hour. He wanted to make sure there was no correlation between his visit and the boy's venturing out. Satisfied that all would be taken care of, he found his staff, blew out the boy's candle, and left him to the small room and the sounds of the other squire's breathing.

*　　*　　*

Ruben lay awake under his covers, incensed at the gall of the codger that had just left the room. *This is really happening*, he realized incredulously. The conspiracy they had suspected was going on had just proven itself to be true. The squire made himself count to one thousand before getting out of bed to set their plan in motion. He didn't want to accidently run into the limping herbologist on his way to rat him out. He looked down at the younger boy that he had previously seen as a thorn in his side, and now admired for his bravery. When this was all said and done, he would be a worthy friend to have.

He snuck out of the room quietly. He now understood why Cal had been so clumsy and tired all the time recently. He thought Cal deserved to get as much rest as he could before the herbologist's commands triggered in the boy's head. Having him sit there like that was just cruel. However, if Ruben had known more about Master Zalice's tricks on the mind, he would have understood that if Cal had fallen into a natural sleep, the trance would have been broken.

Ruben headed to the barracks where Ormond and Sir Stanton were waiting. The king and queen had gone away on urgent business of their own, so Ormond and Stanton had been apprised of the situation, and had been put in charge of the operation. At first, Stanton had been angry that the boys hadn't come to him first, but King Oslan had talked to the knight, and had smoothed things over for the boys.

Ruben felt honored to be working with the general. The squire had been in the service of Sir Stanton for so long, that he had met Ormond on several occasions. Ruben had a deep respect for the man as a tactical expert, and his bravery was a trait Ruben thought he shared. He didn't feel the need to gush as the younger boy did, he was much older after all, but he could admit that he felt better knowing the plan was in his hands.

Ormond had been given the location of the council members, and was able to tell Ruben where to go to find Calen. The general also sent a messenger to tell the knights guarding that area of the town not to attack the small intruder that they were expecting.

The first target was a Carrier of Brightness, or rather, the temple's vault which held the wanderers' things. These were a sect of travellers that brought hope and wisdom to the downtrodden and poorer folk of the kingdom. They were known for their generosity, and had worked with the kings of the ages to make sure everyone was fed and clothed if they could not afford to do so for themselves.

Ruben got to the temple and had to wait what seemed to be an eternity for one of the Carriers to be summoned to the door of the tent. He refused to talk with Ruben about the situation until Ruben had assured him that he was happy and well taken care of by Sir Sprig. Finally, the Carrier allowed the conversation to be turned to the expected intruder.

To Ruben's chagrin, Cal had already come and gone. No one had stood in his way, but it had taken a while for the boy to locate where the signet ring of the temple was located. It seemed as if everything was falling far behind schedule. This made Ruben nervous, and a feeling of dread started to creep into his nerves. Every second that stretched out through the night brought Cal closer to being discovered by people waking to do their early morning chores at sunrise.

Chapter 35
✪ Caught in the Act ✪

Ruben excused himself from his meeting with the Carrier of Brightness, and headed to Cal's second mark, a rich man named Thormyn.

Thormyn was a wealthy tavern and inn owner who thought he knew better than everyone else. Ruben had met the man before when Sir Stanton had been conducting some business in the capital. Ruben had found the man to be pompous and overbearing. The squire had half a mind to leave the man to his own devices, but it was Cal that he was really going for.

Ruben made his way to Thormyn's Spacious Satchel, one of the up-scale inns in Endalwynndale. You had to have money to stay there, and it was usually occupied by wealthy travelling merchants, or special guests of the more prominent nobles. The food was rumoured to always be cooked to perfection, thanks to the man's daughter, Molly. There was always a bard or minstrel for entertainment, and the rooms were considered to be the most luxurious next to the castle itself. In this part of town it was the place to be, if you could afford it.

Ruben raced there as fast as his legs could carry him. The meeting with Ormond and Sprig had taken longer than he had anticipated, and he had already missed Cal at the temple. With the sky beginning to lighten, Ruben wasn't sure what scenario he would be walking into. Cal could be in very real danger if he was caught. Ruben just hoped that Thormyn was still asleep, and that there would be no hitch in Cal's undertakings.

When Ruben arrived, horror swept through

him. He looked up to the roof, where Calen stood teetering on the steep incline, the herbologist's black pouch dangling from one hand. Thormyn was facing him while wielding a sharp dagger, and he was shrieking his head off to alert the guards. On the ground below, one of the castle's knights hesitantly held a light crossbow aimed at Cal's back. Ruben thought the man had received Ormond's orders; otherwise, he would have already taken the very clear shot.

"What are you waiting for?" Thormyn yelled, "Shoot the thief!"

A window below the encounter opened as one of the guests awoke to the noise and realized that something was amiss. *No,* Ruben thought urgently, *there has to be something I can do.* Every new pair of eyes that bore witness to this held the potential to endanger Cal's life.

He looked around for something that could help. For now, the guard wasn't shooting, but there was still the danger of Calen falling from the second story roof. He saw a horse saddled to a cart full of hay. Likely, it was to be delivered to the stables for when the stable boys had mucked out the stalls.

He ordered the guard to lead the horse and cart over to the base of the building. He would kill two birds with one stone this way. He would provide a safer place for Cal to land, and the cart would block the back door of the establishment, preventing nosey patrons from exiting and potentially making the situation more difficult.

As the guard gathered the horse's reins, Ruben shot in through the back door, and ran up the stairs to the open window leading to the roof. He leaned out and looked up to where the two figures stood.

"Thormyn, stop, you were given orders from

the king and queen!" Ruben declared.

The inn keeper sneered "Please, Oslan has been king for all of a day. Do you really think that he knows how to properly run a kingdom? If his idea is to allow a thief to run rampant in his land, then I for one hope that he and the queen are gone for some time. Sometimes, one has to take matters into one's own hands."

Ruben was shocked. "This is treason", he remarked.

"You're Sprig's squire, aren't you? Yes, I think so. Does he know that you're trespassing here? Did you pay for the room you just came through? As far as I'm concerned, the both of you should be locked up! What kind of house is *Sir* Stanton running anyhow?" he mocked rudely.

Ruben saw red. He drew his own sword from his belt. "You will drop your dagger, or I will arrest you myself and report your behaviour to Ormond before the day is out," he threatened. He prayed that it would work.

"Alright boy, I'll drop my knife," he said a little too congenially. His eyes shifted to Cal, and the man lunged at him, throwing his deadly blade.

Ruben watched helplessly as Cal lurch away from the strike and he and the man both began to slide down the steep incline to the bottom edge of the roof.

Whatever was controlling Cal's actions, whether it be instincts or hypnosis, took over and the new squire did a neat back flip out and down as he reached the edge of the roof. He was able to land in a hand-stand on the balcony rail of the window beneath the one Ruben leaned out of. Ruben felt a hint of jealousy creep in to accompany his sense of relief.

Thormyn had been higher on the roof and as

he slid past the gable of Ruben's window, he made a reach for the window sill. He missed the white wooden sill, but grabbed Ruben's shirt, pulling him out of the window as the inn keeper slid by.

"Help!" Ruben called reflexively as the end of the roof and the ground below rushed up towards him. Ruben wouldn't have believed it, and even afterwards couldn't understand how the actions of the next few moments were even possible. Cal's subconscious must have picked up on the verbal cue of "help", and he had simply acted. One minute Ruben was plummeting through space, and the next, he was grabbed by one small hand.

There he hung, suspended beside the balcony as the smaller squire balanced on the other hand. Ruben could see the veins on the side of Cal's neck and face bulge. Ruben understood that the muscles, tendons and ligaments in Cal's arm were trying to support his substantial weight. He remembered that Cal hadn't even been able to hold up Sir Stanton's mail, and he wondered if the boy's shoulder had dislocated in the rescue.

"By the shields of the army of Ormond, boy, don't let go!" Thormyn begged. He still hung from Ruben's shirt, though that had started to rip. Ruben took a moment to look down, then spoke to Thormyn.

"Oh don't worry, he won't," he reassured the ignoramus right before using his sword to slice through the rest of the fabric that held the man.

The air was filled with a high pitched scream not unlike the squeals of a maid terrified by a mouse. Ruben watched to make sure Thormyn landed safely in the cart of hay below as he had planned. The annoying man landed squarely in the middle of the soft hay and his squawking stopped. That was when Ruben realized that the inn keeper now had possession of the black bag. *Cal must have released it in order to save me*, Ruben realized. *I have to get it back!*

Ruben swung his sword arm up to grasp the edge of the balcony so Cal could let go. He heard a cackle of triumph. Ruben looked down below his dangling feet as the staff-bearing herbologist limped onto the scene below. As the bewildered Thormyn crawled out of the straw, Ruben watched Augden Zalice spirit the pouch out of the inn keeper's hand.

"Seize that man!" Ruben called down to the guard. Unfortunately, with both hands now hugging the rail of the balcony, he had no way of indicating which man he meant. He looked down again to make sure that when he let go, he too would fall into the hay.

Fractions of a second before he was able to let go, a violent blast of heat followed by the chill of ice pierced Ruben to the bone. Alarmingly, he found he couldn't move a single muscle; it was if they had all turned to stone. His mind couldn't wrap itself around what had happened to them. The sun was now up and many people had begun their day. From what Ruben could see without being able to shift his gaze, everyone on the ground was in the same predicament. *What is this? Did something go wrong with the queen's magic? No, the queen is away. Are we under attack?* As far as he knew, Augden Zalice had no magical abilities, and the herbologist seemed to be frozen too. *At least he won't be able to get away,* Ruben consoled himself.

Eventually, Ruben had formulated a new plan to catch the man, in case this was ever undone. He had tried to flex every muscle in his body, but they had seemed disjointed, as if his mind and body were no longer connected. So he hung there like a clumsy gargoyle that had fallen off its perch.

Unmoving, Ruben began to count the seconds into minutes, the minutes into hours, and the hours until the numbers began to lose meaning for him. Finally, he lost count, and eventually when the light dimmed again, he slept.

Chapter 36
☼ Chosen ☼

Lazelan squeezed his eyes shut and strained his floor-pressed ear, but still he heard nothing new. He pictured his young wife's beautiful face, and was glad she would be his last thought.

"Is it over yet?" he heard Harmonium ask.

"Not yet, but soon," was Wolfbane's reply.

Lazelan felt something solid brush roughly across his body, and found that now the sound of the moving wall was coming from his other side.

"That's it," Wolfbane reported, "you can move now."

Lazelan lifted his wet ear off the tile he had been listening to. He was confused. "Move?" he asked the gnome. "Master, I still have not heard what you wanted me to. I think I have an idea, but we have to be quick, and I can't see. I think I might have found a way out, but I need to hear the riddle again."

"Aelesra eyt elahae. Gol tax rau dir lan uta, lan Sae postik faltimiyat. Jehaol, yesra umek Ey." *Welcome my guests. There is no need for that, for you have succeeded. Please, come with me.* A deep and smooth voice like silk intoned from across the room.

How? Lazelan was trying to work out. Only moments before Lazelan would have sworn there had existed no way in or out, but clearly the man had come from somewhere. Lazelan stood, opening and shutting his eyes repeatedly, still trying to lift the white cloudy veil that was impeding his vision.

"Let me help," insisted his master's voice. Lazelan heard Harmonium approach, and felt the heat of the palm of his master's hand on his face. Then, coolness washed over his eyes, and a new veil of blue carried away the damage. Harmonium removed his hand, the blue faded, and once again, Lazelan could see clearly.

"Thank you," he said earnestly in a very relieved voice. Lazelan followed the sound of the wall, as it finished moving across the room. Now he understood what had happened. The bottom layer of stones was cut out of the wall, which had allowed it to pass over them as they lay on the ground.

"The riddle's answer was *fall*," the gnome told him. He still held the scimitar in his injured hand, but now the flame had gone out.

"Your hand!" Lazelan exclaimed, remembering the awful sound and smell of the injury taking place.

"It doesn't hurt anymore," Wolfbane told him as if unbelieving himself.

"Jehaol, xa tax raux kras ot faktim so fai milom." *Please, it is not wise to keep the princess waiting.* The same new voice informed them, slightly impatiently this time.

Lazelan looked over at a new wall that had been hidden behind the moving facade of the trap. He saw an opened doorway with a pointy arched top. Standing where the door should have been was a man with tight curly hair as black as obsidian, and dark skin the likes of which the mage had never seen. The man wore naught but beige voluminous pants made of a light flowing fabric similar to the one used to form Lazelan's shirt. The man's pants ballooned out around his legs and were gathered at the ankles. A fabric belt tied several times around his waist held a curved sheath tucked under one of its folds. His left ear bore two small holes, one in the lobe and the other at the top, that were linked by a golden chain with four blue beads.

The urgency of a rushing wave from the sea

crept into his voice, yet he stood as still as a snowy peak on Mount Embalk that had sat in place for a thousand years, and would still be there for a thousand yet to come.

"Nae postik ot gallot e, jehaol." *We have to go now, please.*

"Who is this guy, and what is he saying?" Wolfbane asked.

Lazelan felt bad for not remembering that the gnome would be clueless to what was going on.

"He wants us to follow him." Lazelan replied. "I don't know who he is."

The man led them under the doorway and through a corridor. Wall sconces held burning torches for them to see by. Lazelan's curiosity was brimming. The man walked completely erect with a straight spine, and so smoothly that he almost seemed to float. As he walked, he pulled the sheath from his belt and turned to hand it down to Wolfbane.

"Tay taja dir uti.Rau sult taxa klip so xriel nula so fai umek tarit artamiyat liltot." *You will need this. No one may enter the presence of the princess with an exposed blade.*

Harmonium translated for Wolfbane, and then warned Lazelan in the common tongue. "Until we leave this pyramid, pretend that you have forgotten all you know about magic."

"What? Why?" Lazelan asked.

"The Embralish believe in complete and utter subservience to their ruler. If you should accidently cast in front of her without her permission, it would mean instant death."

"Utter sub-what?" Wolfbane asked.

"It means that the people under her rule show complete unquestioning obedience."

"Wait, he's a slave?" Wolfbane tried to

confirm while gesturing at the man they followed.

"Not exactly," Harmonium answered. "The people here love their matriarch so much that their culture dictates that being chosen to serve her is a great honor. Men that become Jarusiyat, or Chosen, are happy to do the work they do, because they feel honored that it was them that was asked to do the job. Even menial tasks like washing her feet, or fetching something for her is a treasured undertaking."

"That um...sounds special." Wolfbane finished.

Harmonium continued, "That's actually a very good word for it. The Embralish are also known as the omen people. The desert gets its name from its inhabitants. Embra means omen in Almatrae. They see omens in just about everything, which is why it is important we don't break any of their laws. Anything can be construed as having another meaning, which is one reason their social structure works as well as it does. A man asked to sop up the matriarch's spilt wine for example, will feel empowered to have been chosen. The spilt wine might be seen as a sign that disaster is imminent, or that the people will suffer a loss. But others will see the chosen's completed task as an omen that he is able to rectify any messy situation that may occur. He will gain standing in their society. This is why they live to serve, and are happy to do it."

"What about us?" Wolfbane asked. "What are the chances that they will keep us as one of these chosen?"

"That is not what we need to fear here." Harmonium told him. "The Embralish people are very particular, and we won't fit in. They only concern themselves with beings that they consider to be pure. They speak only Almatrae, and won't sully their mouths with other spoken tongues. All we have to worry about is not offending the princess so we can get out of this pyramid alive.

Chapter 37
☼ Hand Me Down ☼

The four men walked out of the corridor and into a room that was huge. A waterfall that ended in a large rectangular fountain decorated one wall and a section of the floor. It made a pleasant dribbling and splashing that echoed throughout the room. Here and there, they saw more men like the one that had led them in.

All of the men appeared to be in their prime. They all sported impressive muscles, had the same tight curls, and wore the same billowy pants. They appeared to be around the same height but their skin tones ranged from the light colour of one of Aylan's teas to the dark brown of dried cloves. The only other difference Lazelan could see about them was the number of blue beads that dangled from the chains that adorned their ears.

In the middle of them all was a tall alabaster throne carved in swirling columns that reached well above the heads of anyone standing in the room. Around the throne, stood four men waving wide leaves of a fern to create a cool breeze for its occupant.

Upon the cushioned royal seat sat a woman of incredible beauty. Gold threads coiled around some of her tight curls as they fanned out around her face and shoulders. She wore a series of golden chains around her neck, all adorned with the same blue beads that the men wore in their ears. Her loose robe was of the same breathable material as the men's pants. It covered only one shoulder and was synched at the waist with a wrapped around belt like the men's. The material on her shoulder was clasped in a broach to let the end hang down her back.

She noticed the group of men enter from the hall and lifted a hand. Instantly, everyone in the throne room sunk face down to the ground. There they waited, as she watched to see if the foreigners would comply. Lazelan was aware of Harmonium sinking to the floor beside him, and followed suit.

"Get down!" Lazelan hissed at the gnome, who was now the only one standing. Oblivious, Wolfbane was trying to sheath the scimitar as the Chosen one had warned, but the gnome still hadn't managed to put the thing away. It was still in his hand and he looked like he was struggling with it. Lazelan hoped that the princess wouldn't take it as an affront.

"I'm sorry, your highness," Wolfbane started to address her.

A whispered phrase, "Taxa Tayt xuae aeles sparkra,"*May your ears remain pure,* passed through the room. Lazelan didn't think it was possible, but the men in the room all seemed to sink even closer to the ground. The princess didn't wait for the gnome to finish.

"Trimas," *Rise,* she commanded in a regal voice. "Sae taxa yesat," *You may approach,* she allowed.

Suddenly, they were surrounded by a circle of the Chosen. Lazelan and Harmonium were ushered toward the throne. Everyone in the room treated Wolfbane as if he wasn't even there. Her bright eyes danced over her high cheek bones. Her thick lips curved into a smile that said she already knew the answer to the question she was about to ask.

"Kelda sult nula sae postik postiyat Eay eyt filtot?" *Which one of you has brought me my sword?* She asked. She looked excitedly from one mage to the other. Her smile quickly faded as she noticed their empty bare hands.

"sinatayt taelah postik xa," *Our friend has it,* Lazelan told her, motioning to Wolfbane to help explain. Lazelan thought she looked taken aback.

"Bod uta tax sauxraot," *But that is impossible,* she announced. Lazelan dared not contradict her. He watched as she strode quickly to where the gnome was standing. This time, Wolfbane seemed to have enough sense to bow low in front of the princess, but he looked like a rabbit caught in a trap.

Lazelan pointed to his hand, and then made small swiping motions like he was fighting with a sword. Wolfbane understood, and offered her the scabbard, although his hand was still tightly wrapped around the hilt. When she tried to take it, the sword unsheathed, and the brilliant flame once again flared to life between them.

What are you doing? Lazelan silently mouthed across the room. *You can't brandish a weapon at the princess! Drop it!* He made an opening hand gesture, and the gnome's fingers opened. He began to flick his hand about as if he was trying to rid it of the sword that wouldn't budge. *I can't!* he mouthed back dramatically.

"Tabox," *Enough,* her voice was like a storm, as it grew more forceful and unpredictable. "Gollit nae, arat so rik," *Leave us, clear the room.*

Every one of the Chosen had filed out of the room in mere seconds. Lazelan was impressed. Impressed, and frightened. The princess looked around, presumably to check that there were none of her men left in the room. She must have been satisfied, because she knelt in front of Wolfbane then. She moved the dagger in its scabbard to the opposite side of his sword belt, and added the curved sheath of the scimitar that she held in her hand.

"You may put the sword away," she said haltingly, her very thick accent almost making it impossible to tell that she was speaking the common tongue. Lazelan was stunned and he could tell that it was difficult for her. It came out like *"Yo-u mah-ee poot teh swor-id awah-ee."*

"But I thought you couldn't speak common," Wolfbane challenged her as he sheathed the scimitar. His hand came away freely now. She took it, and studied the markings branded into his skin from the fire.

"I cannot," she replied in her broken common tongue.

"But you are speaking it right now," Wolfbane pushed. She gave him a piercing look.

"If I were to ever utter even a single word in anything but the great language in front of my Chosen, I would have to slay them all," she explained, "This is the way of it."

"Then Princess, you must be great indeed, for I think I am beginning to understand your Almatrae perfectly." He replied.

*   *   *

Almost a week passed. The princess worked with them for hours every day, collecting pieces of spells and antidotes that she had personally added to the missing *Almatraek Bright*. She had been one of its authors, and knew what lay within some of its pages.

While they worked, the Chosen were kept away from the princess for their own safety. The only exception to the rule was a man named Xander, who seemed to be able to come and go with things the queen requested. Lazelan understood, for him that would have been Magdolyn, the one person he trusted completely. Lazelan had befriended and liked the man, and he knew he would actually miss him when they had departed.

The other members of the Chosen seemed to eye Lazelan and his friends almost defiantly when the princess wasn't around. Lazelan had ventured to ask Xander about it, and he had replied that the other members of the Chosen were anxious for the group to move on. After all, the presence of Lazelan and his friends was keeping the men from being able to serve their princess.

Finally, the party had collected what they needed. Lazelan was surprised that no one had batted an eye at Wolfbane carrying around the sheathed scimitar, and he was even more surprised that the princess was allowing him to keep it. Since the Chosen were being kept away so the princess could communicate with Wolfbane, Lazelan had seen them talking often, and thought that they had developed a new respect for each other.

Wolfbane explained to Lazelan later that he had been unable to drop the sword at first; it had stuck to his palm like pollen does to a bee. He had shown Lazelan his newly branded palm, which bore a single word in Almatrae: *Jarusiyat*. Lazelan had opted not to tell his friend that the word inscribed on it meant *Chosen*.

On one afternoon when the gnome had been elsewhere, Lazelan had asked Princess Xinavane about it. She told him that since Wolfbane had chosen to save the sword, the sword had chosen the gnome. Their spirits were now linked. It would be with the gnome now until his death. She told him that it had nothing to do with holding a position of servitude in the pyramid. Lazelan didn't know if that would have been the case if it had been one of the mages that spoke Almatrae that had rescued the sword. Either way, that was good enough for the mage.

On the eve before their departure, Lazelan was talking with the princess in the throne room when the sound of music began to lift from the fountain. Xinavane explained that it was a warning spell, letting them know that someone was attempting to scry them.

He knew it was a long shot, but Lazelan raced to one of the light reflecting disks on the wall. He tried to scry Aylan, and sure enough, there she was, standing beside her king. Lazelan grinned like a young boy who had been given a sweet, and stepped back so Xinavane could meet his former pupil. It was the first time he had seen Aylan in her role as queen, and as she conducted herself, he felt a strong sense of pride. After all, as her former teacher, he had helped her become the capable person she was now.

He learned from Aylan that the people of Endalwynndale had been struck by folly. Everyone in the kingdom seemed to be locked into place by some stony spell. He had no idea what it could be, but by enlisting the princess' help, they found a spell that Xinavane thought might work to free them. Unfortunately, it seemed to be yet another riddle, and one the king and queen would have to figure out for themselves.

Lazelan was determined to set off with his friends again on the morrow. He had enjoyed the last few days in the triangular shaped fortress. It had seemed safe and simple here. The princess had kindly suggested a small list of other mages that might be of some help, though she knew not whether they were still alive. She had given him copies of some of the spells that she had written into the *Almatraek Bright* many years before. She suggested that if the trail became a dead end, he might be able to begin compiling spells to create a new book of brightness. Either way, with her spells in his possession, Lazelan had grown more confident that their quest might actually succeed, and Endalwynndale might be free of evil once and for all.

They supped in private with Xinavane and Xander on their last night in the pyramid. The princess told them that they were always welcome back. In the morning, her Chosen man, Xander, would show them a direct and safe path out of the pyramid that would bypass all of the deadly traps.

In what might be the last time Xinavane was ever to speak the common tongue, the princess made a request, "If you do succeed in this quest young mage, I ask that you all swear yourselves to secrecy about what you have seen and heard here. The mysteries of the kingdom that dwells within the desert cannot be lost to the outside world."

They gave their assurances that they would not betray any of the secrets of the society of the Chosen or the fortress in which she lived.

"After all," she added, "I have to make certain that my *pyramid* will remain in good *shape*."

Lazelan and Harmonium frowned down at Wolfbane, who beamed up at the princess in pride.

"What's the point in speaking a language," he gloated, "if you can't have pun with it?"

Chapter 38
✿ Coming Around ✿

Cal awoke to find the world had turned upside down. He was somewhere high up, and he felt totally disoriented with no clue as to where he was. *Am I hanging by my feet or something?* he wondered. He also wanted to know how their plan from the other night had ended up like this. He remembered drinking Master Zalice's brew, and watching the coin flick across his fingers. Eventually, sleep had taken him.

His first reflex was to call for help. He tried, and was filled with a sense of complete and utter terror when he found he could not. He began to panic. His head wouldn't budge, so he could not even survey the scene, nor could he move any of his limbs. He might have begun to shake or cry if he had been able to, but he was only able to remain upside down, thinking of his predicament.

It was as if the connection from his mind to his body had been cut off. There was no feeling in his arms, and no fatigue in his muscles, but gradually he came to realize that he had been supporting himself. *What was I thinking? Was I crazy?* his mind reeled. He contemplated how he could have even gotten there, and decided that perhaps his target had been the occupant of the room with the balcony he was perched on.

He remained there, thinking and figuring, trying to piece it all together. There was always an advantage to any situation, and since he was stuck there, he tried to find it. *At least I don't have to worry about falling*, he reasoned, except he feared what would happen when whatever this was wore out. He wasn't sure if his muscles would be able to hold him, or how he would safely get down.

The light and dark of days passing into nights in their endless cycle rolled around again and again, but he hadn't kept track of how many times. For the first few changes, they had come and gone in complete silence. Then he had heard hushed voices, and the clanging of knights wearing armour travelling the streets.

At first he felt elated, finally, someone had come to save them! Hope surged up within him, and he prayed that the brightness would light their way to a solution, whoever they were. But then nothing had happened. He waited, still expectant, but with his anticipation of a rescue dropping a little with each passing minute.

It had been hours since he had heard the voices. Perhaps they had no answers. Maybe they had been captured. It was possible they had tried and failed, and he would be left like this forever. He began to wonder morbidly if he would ever die, or if he would just rest like this, till the end of days.

He saw movement at the edge of his vision. A shadow moved, and the squawking roar of a prehistoric beast filled the skies. Moments later the shadow returned and with it came the heat of a thousand suns. Fire rained down and enveloped Calen for a breath of time, cracking through the stony spell. Then the fire was gone and Cal's muscles, now exhausted as if they had held up the world, gave out.

He fell from the second story balcony, and savoured the cry that was now able to rip from his lungs. He landed in the hay, and forced his muscles to move when he saw Ruben dropping from the sky right after him. He tried to stand, but his legs had fallen asleep. He toppled unceremoniously out of the cart. Luckily for him some poor fool happened to be where he landed, so once again there was something soft to break his fall.

"Get off me, boy!" Master Zalice fumed. Evidently, he had been trying to make an escape.

"I'm sorry, Master Zalice, I can't, my legs don't seem to be working," Cal shared.

"Wait until Sir Stanton hears about this!" the herbologist blustered.

"I think that's a wonderful idea," Ruben said, now standing in the cart. "In fact, why don't we go see him right now?"

Cal beamed up at the older squire, who winked at him conspiratorially. For the first time since starting his new job, Cal actually felt like he had done something important and right.

Chapter 39
☼ Loose Ends ☼

The guard that had been responsible for moving the cart of hay for Ruben offered to escort them to Ormond and Sprig to make sure Augden Zalice would go along. Cal hadn't been sure how he was going to force the herbologist to turn himself in, and even with Ruben's help, he doubted they could have dragged the man to the palace themselves. Luckily, the guard had seen Augden take the pouch out of Thormyn's hand after the fall, and had thought that reporting it was a good idea. Cal was relieved that it was now all over.

When they got to the barracks, Cal was shocked to find the place empty. He worried that another spell might be at work. *Where is everyone? Were they at war right now with the magical culprit that had sent the kingdom into stillness?* he tried to deduce.

The four of them went to the keep and thankfully found the door guarded. The servants and most of the knights had all been summoned to the throne room to help clean up a massive amount of destruction that had resulted from Queen Aylan's battle with two mages. An old foe, Zaltreous, and a noble named Aurastia had tried to claim the throne for themselves in the king and queen's absence.

Cal was flabbergasted upon entering what used to be the throne room. He could tell that the servants would be working for a long time to repair the extensive damage done to the tapestries, furniture, and even the furrowed stone floor.

A group of nobles huddled in the corner. They had been frozen there when the magical blast had hit, and the evil mages had handled them roughly to get the inconvenient bodies out of their way. Some sported injuries from the magical duel, and others were just in shock. Augden rushed over to help where he could. Cal didn't have a problem with that, as long as the scoundrel didn't try to sneak out of the room.

King Oslan had thought that Augden was responsible for the chaos in his kingdom. The guard testified that he had caught Augden with the pouch, which contained all of the seals now stamped into the red wax. Ruben came forward to tell the king about the fact that Augden had been frozen along with the rest of them, so he couldn't have been a part of that spell. He also grudgingly told the king about how the man had helped the nobles in the aftermath. It didn't make up for his wrongdoings however.

Cal was a little bitter that things worked out for Augden in the long run. The herbologist had been charged with conspiracy against the council, but his actions to aid the nobles in their time of need had helped to sway the decision about his punishment. Since Aylan had taken to bedrest following her brush with death and ensuing illness, Augden had been charged with seeing to the castle's medical needs, without pay. Perhaps when he had worked off his debt to the council, some of the nobles would keep him on as he had originally intended. As for Calen, the boy had decided that he would never let the herbologist near him again, not even with a ten foot pole...unless it was against him during a jousting match.

King Oslan the Brave had said he was very impressed by the undertakings of Ruben and Cal. The younger squire had many years left of training before he could be knighted, but Calen was happy to learn that both the king and Sir Stanton thought he would do just fine. In a private ceremony later that week, Ruben was dubbed a full-fledged knight. Sir Stanton thought his squire was more than fit, and had not objected when Oslan requested to do the knighting ceremony himself. Ruben had been granted his own lands and could have left House Sprig, but he told Cal that he intended to stay on a bit longer to help put the boy through his paces. Cal was looking forward to showing the new knight what he could do.

☼ Epilogue ☼

The weeks passed into months. By now, the castle's repairs had been completed, and all of the guests that had come for the coronation were long gone. Aylan loved the balls and the feasting the palace held for special occasions; they were always such grand affairs. But she, like the townsfolk, appreciated when life was back to business as usual.

Aylan had been confined to bedrest when her illness had persisted. Her magic wasn't working properly, and it seemed there would be no end to the sick feeling she got multiple times a day. She felt as large and as awkward as a hippo, and strange things had started to happen that she couldn't explain. Whenever they occurred, she found herself to be fatigued and hungry enough to eat a bear.

The shadow of the winged sphinxes came rolling across the countryside, and the townsfolk were terrified. When the giant cats began to circle the castle, the servants started to flee and the knights assembled to take care of the problem.

Of course, the queen had heard about none of this, as Oslan had not wanted to tax her with the news. Instead, he sent for her mother to stay with her, just in case. Millie, her handmaid, would not be cowardly enough to leave the queen's side, and so everything in the bedchambers seemed to be normal. Aylan was in the middle of making a scroll of possible names for the baby with her mother, Lorelyn.

"So far we have Athrusia,Thrushyn, Thrushlynn, Thrushal, and just plain old Thrush," Aylan read off the list they were compiling.

She was interrupted by a series of unsettling heavenly noises. A loud *crack* came from above as the first sphinx alighted on the conical roof of the tower at the front of the castle, its claws ripping off some of the clay tiles as it landed. Aylan began to fear that the castle was under attack. A low rumbling outside her chambers grabbed her attention as the second cat touched down outside the royal couple's chambers, peered inside, and started to purr.

~ The End of Book Three ~

Dear Adventurer,

Thank you for voyaging with Lazelan and his brave party across the golden dunes of the Embralic Desert, and into the depths of the bobby-trapped pyramid of Xinavane. You found out that being an expert at the word games of gnomes is no small feat, and that sometimes a good mind is the best way out of a bad situation. You watched a young boy become a villain and a hero, and saw how dangerous a flip of a coin can be.

Lazelan's search continues as he and his comrades follow the trail of the *Almatraek Bright* to the frigid peaks of Mount Embalk, and the ancient cities within. They must race to find the book before other forces at work can make his trail run cold. Will Sasha be able to see a way around the obstacles put in their place? Meanwhile in Endalwynndale, deadly creatures have come to the castle with a message for the queen. Will they be glad tidings, or a warning of doom that has yet to come?

Till A Quest Calls Again,
Heather Reilly

www.ingramcontent.com/pod-product-compliance
Lightning Source LLC
Chambersburg PA
CBHW070703280626
47159CB00022B/1863